MINOTAUR: BLOODED

The Bestial Tribe

NAOMI LUCAS

Minotaur: Blooded
The Bestial Tribe

By Naomi Lucas

❀ Created with Vellum

Also by Naomi Lucas

Stranded in the Stars

Last Call

Collector of Souls

Star Navigator

Cyborg Shifters

Wild Blood

Storm Surge

Shark Bite

Mutt

Ashes and Metal

Chaos Croc (Coming Soon)

Valos of Sonhadra

Radiant

The Bestial Tribe

Minotaur: Blooded

Book Two (Coming 2019)

Aldora lived in a bordertown on the edge of the maze. A labyrinth that spanned an eternity filled with creatures that howled through the night. She was a daughter of farmers that worked the fields and endured a quiet life as a peasant, away from the capital and its nihilistic celebrations; away from all that would look at her and discern her worth. Because to be chosen as a sacrifice was to be chosen to *die*.

Until one night, while at the maze wall, she heard a husky voice in the darkness.

Vedikus Bathyr.

He prowled the overgrown passages at the farthest edges where the true, intelligent beasts roamed. They were all there for the same reasons: to kill each other and capture the humans that entered the labyrinth.

One fated night a human girl called out to him. A girl with a voice that quickened his blood.

But he wasn't the only one to hear her call...

Chapter One

Aldora adjusted the grip on her burlap satchel. The bag was filled to the brim with supplies from town and a few uneaten apples from her mother's orchard. With every step, its weight bounced against her side. She was sure to have a new bruise before the evening sun crested the horizon.

Her eyes drifted to the purple mottled sky and the night clouds in the distance. They spread out in front of her, unhindered by the dirt path she traversed. On either side were trees, tall, withered and old, and she tried not to focus on them. Their daytime green faded from their leaves to darken with the coming night

Focusing on them would mean acknowledging them and after spending a lifetime living in their shadow, there was little left to frighten her. Now, she only looked upon the trees with curiosity. Aldora breathed in. The aroma of loam and pine filled her nose.

This path and these trees were the perfect backdrop for

a horror story, one that was real, potent, and told to all children to keep them from being...

Children.

Stories of what lurked within the darkness of the trees, and what may be hiding out of sight. The children of her town were made to be afraid of all they could not see or explain. With tales of terror related to the giant wall just beyond.

There were creatures that lived on the other side that wanted to hunt and eat you—or worse—and the only way to appease them was to respect them.

Ghouls, beasts, ghosts, and goblins—all liked to dine on human flesh.

The leaves blew overhead, and she looked up.

Several shadows appeared in the distance ahead of her where the path curved. She hesitated, swallowing, and lowered her head. Voices rose as they drew near.

"Hail, miss," one of the shadows said.

Aldora raised her gaze and tightened her grip on her bag. Two men stood before her. They were uniformed in patrol garb, the red and white of their vests apparent even in the twilight.

Laslites. She released a quiet breath and pulled her unwilling lips into a shy smile.

Aldora couldn't make out their features; the sun was at their back and it spotted her eyesight, distorting her vision just enough to darken their faces. The Laslites could see her though.

"Hail," she responded, bowing her head.

One of the men stepped forward. "It's getting late. Where are you headed at this time of night?"

"Home, sir." She hefted her full bag. "My mother's farm."

"How far is it?" He took another step toward her.

"Before the next crossroads. If I continue on my way, I'll be there before the light is gone."

"Ah! You must live in Ledger. We recently passed their fields." He chuckled. "Go on then, and go fast. The border mists have worsened of late." The Laslite returned to his companion who had begun walking away. Aldora turned around to watch their red and white backs grow smaller in the distance.

"What do you mean they've worsened?" she called out, stopping them. Her eyes moved to the trees at their sides.

"You don't know?" The Laslite canted his head.

Know what? She'd been in town all day delivering orders and selling fruit at the market and hadn't even heard a hushed rumor. Truthfully, she hadn't been listening, but if the mists had worsened… Someone would've been talking about it. Someone would've been afraid.

The Laslite glanced at his companion and dropped his hand to his sword belt. "Burlox, the town south of here, was consumed by the labyrinth, not a fortnight past. And you know, when the mists spread, the labyrinth follows closely behind... Miss," he hesitated at the worried look she flashed him, "are you sure you don't need an escort? The capital is on alert and is determined to stop the expansion. You do know what that means don't you?"

Yes. I need to get home. Aldora shook herself and came to her senses. "I do know and remain ever vigilant. I pray to the gods every hour for respite, for me and mine, but also for Savadon. I should be fine without an escort." Without waiting for a response, she turned away. "Good day," she said quickly and hastened her step without looking back.

More sacrifices. That, she had known. Other bordertowns had already begun preparations, and even now, criminals were being delivered from the capital to be given to the labyrinth in appeasement.

But the fall of an entire town?

Burlox was a bordertown like her own Thetras. She didn't know much about it except that Burlox bordered the swamp, and that the roads running along the labyrinth were infrequently traveled there.

The soggy land, predators, and marsh fever deterred even the most tenacious patrollers and adventurers.

Those that journeyed to Thetras afterward loved to boast of their courage in surviving the swamp people. Thetras, thankfully, had not been affected yet, and had not received criminals.

They had not made a sacrifice since the last harvest, several months prior, and they had never, in her lifetime, had an issue with the mists spreading.

She'd never been more than several hours outside of Thetras, and even then, Aldora hated leaving it. Travel time was wasted time as far as she was concerned, and having to journey days to get someplace seemed absurd. Everything she could ever want was right here.

She shifted her bag onto her other shoulder, rolling the previous ache away. The sun was moving below the horizon now, and the chatter of nocturnal creatures quickly filled her ears.

I still have a distance to go. Her eyes drifted to the rising moon. *If I run, I can still make it before full dark.* Her tired muscles and clouded head argued otherwise, so she settled on expending her last threads of energy with a brisk walk.

A gut-wrenching roar filled her ears, and dozens of birds shot into the sky, *squawking* with fear.

Aldora startled, stepping back, feeling the blood drain from her face. She clutched her bag to her chest. One hand dropped to the dagger strapped to her hip and jerked it out, brandishing it in the direction of the sound.

She fell back another step, and then another until she was off the path and in the shade of the trees. The grunting, hollering, and shrieking sounds continued and she lowered down into a crouch. Her heart thundered, and she felt the pounding in her chest right down to the soles of her feet. Sweat slickened her palms.

She stared in the direction of the noises, where the trees looked different from those that covered her. Their leaves were half-withered and their trunks covered in vines. The walls of the world labyrinth stood beyond, casting an even deeper shadow.

Even now as the ruckus lessened, she knew it came from behind the thick hedges and crumbling walls. They were bestial, and all bestial things came from one place: *the mist.*

Aldora lowered her dagger and eased her breath. The quieter the noises became, the quieter she became. Soon, what had been the rage of battle became the screams of the dying, and the rasps of the victor.

She squinted as the sunlight dimmed and tucked her dagger back within its sheath, quietly rising to her feet.

Aldora gingerly stepped back onto the path. A grunt sounded and she stilled again. It continued into gruff

5

words and hissed out breaths, all of it husky and deep. Her ears pricked, and she approached the wall to hear it better.

It was the first time she'd ever heard anything remotely sentient so close to the barrier. The usual noises that ascended from the maze were animalistic.

This was still animalistic but… *different.*

She slowly crossed to the other side of the path until she stood at the treeline, peering through the shadowy brush to the wall of the labyrinth hidden behind.

She placed her hand on a nearby trunk and ducked under a branch, moving steadily closer to where the racket originated from. Needles from the vines scraped her skin, protruding twigs snagged her clothes, and the soles of her boots sank down into the moist pile of leaves beneath her feet. Threads of her brown hair were pulled from her braids to tangle in the winding shrubs.

The wall was a living, ever-changing entity but the one thing that was consistent throughout its entirety was the mist that seeped from above and below. It spread like smoke and silk across the barrier, and over the ruins and hedge-growth that made it up. It wasn't dangerous, being so close to the wall. Nothing but the mist could pass through it, but it rarely reached farther than the edge of the path. At least, never near Thetras.

But they sacrificed a lot to the maze. A lot. Hoping it would never try to expand and consume them.

A shiver raked up her spine.

"May your spark reach the light and your body remain untouched."

Aldora stopped. *A voice?* She cocked her head, straining

to hear more, her braids falling forward to rest loosely on her shoulders.

"May your blood nourish the ground and find new life. Blood guard us, blood sustain, until the day that only blood remains."

A breath escaped her as words—rough and deep, but as clear as day—filled her ears. *Someone in the labyrinth is still alive!*

Her satchel landed on the ground with a heavy thud, snapping several sticks under its weight.

"I can hear you!" Aldora shouted, exhilarated, forgetting her fear. "I hear you!"

The rustling noises came to a sudden stop.

No one ever hears voices from the labyrinth. Her eyes widened at the prospect. *Not unless it's during a day of sacrifice.* After that, it was the braying of the terrified, the cries of the innocent, and even those pleas of the guilty rose up like a wicked storm for all to hear.

"Can you hear me? Please hear me." Her eyes darted around. "Are you all right?" She looked for leverage, for something, anything, to use to help her get the man out. It had to be a man. The voice she'd heard was far too harsh and low to be a woman's.

"Hello?" Aldora called out again. The continued silence made her nervous, and the longer it lasted, the more she doubted ever hearing a voice on the other side. All she knew was that if she was on the other side of the wall, and she had survived long enough to catch someone's attention, she'd hope they would try to help her as well.

The warnings and tales of monsters were one thing, but it was the powerful men and women that ruled the last remaining land of sunlight that frightened her the most. Savadon. They had dominion over Thetras, controlled by the town's Master, Nithers Emen, who followed the orders of the Master of the Western Region.

The Masters had the power to pick you out of a crowd and kill you, and those that fought back, the families and friends, were often sacrificed next.

Aldora and her younger sisters had grown up watching the events as children and were taught early on to blend into the crowd, always be pleasant, always make other people need you, and to never allow yourself to stand out.

Because to be noticed... The innocent, the pure, the beautiful and coy often made the best sacrifices to the world maze. It was why Aldora tried to be anything but.

She swallowed and looked up. A canopy of brush and vines half shielded the night sky and she craned her neck to find the top of the wall. Firebugs twinkled in the darkest parts.

"I heard you," she called out one last time, wiping her hands against her leggings. "I hope *your* spark reaches the light and your body remains untouched..."

"Human." A guttural voice filled her ears, startling her anew. "Woman. You give me burial rights and I am not yet dead."

That voice... Her mouth parted in shock. It was dark and wicked. "I didn't know. They seemed like a kind sentiment," she responded quickly, her skin prickling with gooseflesh. "But if you were giving them..."

"If I were giving them then it means that there's a corpse at my feet," he finished for her, his voice deepening still.

8

She paused. *Who had he killed?* "Was it a beast?"

"Woman, I am the beast."

Her gaze zeroed in on the thickly shrouded hedge before her.

I am safe. Nothing that was not human has ever made it across. "I never knew the monsters in the maze could speak our tongue." *His voice is* human. It was rich and mesmerizing, and tickled her ears. Aldora shivered despite herself. She frowned slightly. But then again she'd never heard anything but howls and hisses coming from the labyrinth, and she had walked the border road countless times, on countless days, throughout her whole life.

"Have you met many of us, female?"

"Only you," she whispered.

"That explains your courage in giving me your voice. If you knew us, you'd flee to your woolen pallet and sing through the night that we would not come after you," he taunted with a hint of sinister glee.

I should go. Her fingers twitched. She glanced down at her bag. "You cannot breach the walls. There'll be no fleeing on my part, from you nor the other monsters. You can't chase me down."

There was a momentary silence. Aldora shifted on her feet uneasily.

"Ah, and I yearn to do so."

A warm thrill bloomed. It started as a blush that spread to her core, lower still to the tips of her toes. She clenched them in the confines of her shoes. She was not as afraid as she should be. Any sane person would've run home the moment they heard a sound from the other side, but she found herself intrigued. Maybe because she knew so little about what existed in the labyrinth, and the little bit of knowledge she gained from this interaction could help her in the future.

Maybe because she detested and feared the sacrifices made to it and the night terrors of her youth.

"I have frightened you. Good. But if only I could smell you. There is nothing like the smell of fear."

"I'm not frightened." The more he spoke, the less she was.

"No, which is unusual for a human. If you are so fearless, why not breach the labyrinth and face me? Test the limits of your courage and face your opponent?" The beast laughed, the chill in it slithered over her flesh. "I am willing."

Aldora ignored his goading. "I won't be tricked by you."

"Who's there!?" A new voice filled the twilight.

She twisted around and backed up into the heavy, half-dead foliage of the labyrinth as footsteps approached. The creature at her back had gone quiet. "I heard you, lass! Come out now or pay the price." *A path guard.*

Aldora clamped her mouth shut and gripped the handle of her dagger. *I can't get caught.* A sudden wave of nausea churned her stomach.

She pressed quietly, slowly, for the second time that evening, back into the deepening shade of the trees.

The fear she should've had before now filled her tenfold. Its wormy, slimy, and twitching chill spiked every fiber of her being.

The monsters in the mist were nothing compared to the monsters she lived among. They were brutal with their paranoia, and fast acting when it came to the unknown. She hid from her own kind more than she ever tried to hide from the shadow of the wall. What good was a fiend that couldn't reach you over those that could?

"If you do not want to be caught, female, then I suggest you run," the creature at her back warned, a threatening whisper in the dark. Fear kept her rooted in place.

The patrol drew closer, a hulking figure winding through the trees. *I've made a mistake.* Aldora blinked back tears.

"Run!" the monster hissed.

She surged forward—bolting without thought—her limbs flailing and catching on shrubs. Her entire body created an explosion of noise that served as a beacon for those searching for her.

"Stop right there!" the guard bellowed.

Getting her bearings, she shot through the treeline and onto the path, her feet springing as if she ran across fire. The thudding and pounding of heavy footfalls trailed behind her. He was gaining. And the threats that tore from her pursuer's throat grew closer by the second. The clink of his chain mail was directly behind her.

Her heart raced. She couldn't let him catch her. She dove off the path and back into the trees, this time on the opposite side of the labyrinth and toward Ledger.

I can't go back there! She immediately changed direction. *I can't damn them.* The thought of her family suffering because of her actions terrified her more than being caught. Leaves slapped her face and sticks abraded her skin. The guard continued to bellow, closing in.

"You're under arrest! Once I get my hands on you… Thetras and Savadon will have you!"

A hand came down hard on her shoulder and Aldora swiveled and lowered under its weight. She dodged to the right and ducked her head, keeping one foot in front of the other, but fingers caught in her hair, ripping a lock out. Staggered, she cried out and twisted from the man's grasp, dropping her weapon. She tripped and fell, her knees slamming into the ground as her hand came up to clutch her scalp.

Pain strummed across her scalp.

The man growled as he slammed into her, pressing her into the dead and slimy leaves. Air expelled forcibly from her lungs from his weight. It stunned her briefly but not long enough to give him complete advantage of her. She pushed at the ground and tried to squirm away. He grabbed her braids and snapped her head back.

"It's over you fucking cunt!"

"No!" she shrieked, reaching for her dagger. Her vision swam with stars.

The guard lifted up and forced his knee into her back, his weight locking her in place. "Yes, miscreant whore. I knew something wasn't right about you when you denied my escort. And to find you at the wall… *talking*." He spat on the back of her head.

Tears flooded her eyes. Aldora tilted her face, trying to get a look at the shadowy figure above her. Silvery threads of moonlight filtered through the leaves as she heaved, searching. "Laslite," she gasped. She couldn't see his face but the excess fabric of his uniform piling over the tops of his boots had their color.

He grabbed her hand that had been moving over toward her dagger and wrenched it behind her. She shrieked when another wave of shooting pain burst through her arm. The Laslite gripped the other next and tied them with cord.

"Savadon has no need or use for briar witches," he snarled and jerked the rope binding her wrists, uncaring of strength upon her. She was forced to her feet, screaming. Her arms were stretched behind her and her vision darkened.

"I'm not a witch—" she stammered as quickly as possible.

"Who were you talking to then? A lover? I see no one else. A ghost? That wouldn't help your case." He spun her around to face him, clutching her neck. "Yourself? It matters not. The kingdom can't have its first line of defense playing at treason, even a lowly freeman. If you represent a hole in the kingdom's defenses it is my duty to fill that hole with your corpse."

"I'm innocent! I heard children playing…"

The Laslite's grip on her neck tightened. He stared down at her with contempt as she fought his hold. The rope broke through the skin of her wrists. Air was just out of reach and his hand only tightened further.

"Plea...se…" Aldora wheezed. "I can't…"

The patroller released her and she collapsed, hacking up bile and coughing violently. Her muscles seized.

"I don't believe you, you cunt." He pushed her over with his boot. "But you're a pretty one. A girl who moves that much while being strangled must fight like a wildcat being fucked."

Apprehension knocked the breath right back out of her as his threat filled her head with terrible ideas.

I have to get away. Coughing, she searched for an escape.

The Laslite continued with disdain, "Unfortunately, I can't pass judgment on you alone." The anger in his voice was thick. "Not within Thetras's domain. But those who can are still awake." He crouched and Aldora slowly looked his way. She didn't want to meet his eyes but forced herself to do so, even if she was met with nothing but cruelty.

"I did nothing wrong," she begged.

She'd only been curious about the voice on the other side. The allure of it, and the memory—its deep and melodic threads that had writhed its way into her ears—was replaced with the Laslite's sour breath hitting her nose, filling her with dreadful reality.

Chapter Two

"...why not breach the barrier and test the limits of your courage?" Vedikus taunted, lowering his voice.

"I won't be tricked by you."

Oh, female, but you already have.

Tricked. Lured. Brought forth to the flame, the *unknown*. A *human*. He had not expected a human, let alone a female to hear him say his rites. But now that it had happened and that the fortune of the gray moon looked down upon him, he knew what all his training had been for.

Only the strongest prowled the labyrinth barrier. Only the best hunted for the sacrifices that the humans made. His muscles rippled as sacred blood coursed through his veins.

Vedikus gripped his battle axe and drew it from its sheath. The goblin corpse at his feet, broken from where he wrung its neck and shattered its back, stared up at him with watchful, dead eyes. It had been a scout, or a desperate male looking to start his own pack. It wasn't part of a tribe.

Otherwise, he'd still be locked in battle, fighting off a swarm of them.

Vedikus shook his head and grasped the thick, impenetrable hedge where the human female's voice emanated from. If he wasn't careful, another barrier lurker like himself would get the jump on him and would hear her voice as well.

A call would go out.

He could not let that happen.

She is mine to hunt. His nostrils flared.

No one spoke to the humans on the other side unless it was a witch or a warlock, and those who knew of one guarded their secrets to their grave. Was the female on the other side one? Was she toying with him as if he were a calf? He snorted, and steam released from his nostrils.

The female knows nothing about me. Without looking down, he stepped onto the goblin's head and crushed it beneath his hoof.

He licked his lips, tasting the salt of his sweat bloom on his tongue, and pressed closer to the wall. The mist that surrounded him stung his hand where he touched the barrier, repelling him. Vedikus crushed the vines in his fist and groaned as the pain flowed through him. He...liked pain, almost enjoyed it. It reminded him that he was still alive.

It helped stop his body from overreacting.

I need her to cross.

She was mere feet away, and the only thing that separated them was the hedge and its magic. There was nothing in the labyrinth that could stop him from capturing her...but *this*.

Another bout of steam released from his nose as he looked up the wall until it disappeared into the haze. The vines above danced around, in and out of his sight.

Vedikus sneered, wishing his brother, Astegur, was with him if only for his ingenuity. But as soon as he wished it, he burned the thought away.

Astegur would want her too; he'd fight me for the rights to her. He would not fight his bull brothers if that happened, but he would very much consider it.

They shared females like they shared battle opponents: with bloodthirsty competition, using everything in their arsenal. It mattered not because regardless of who the female was or how pretty her voice, his clan—his brothers —needed her. There were two reasons to scout the dangerous labyrinth walls—to capture the humans that entered and to test your strength against a myriad of opponents.

He was here for the latter with only the *possibility* of a capture but the likelihood was small, not with hundreds of other mist creatures all out for the same thing. At least that's what he told himself.

His brothers, on the other hand, wouldn't deny the fact that they sought human females. They fought for it, every day, honing their skills, driving their willpower hard and their muscles harder to build the stamina and endurance needed for the sacrificial zones. He tensed his body and felt the power he held ignite.

There was no greater prize than a pureblood human,

but he was here to hone his skills and scout the lands, not to seek out and capture a female. *I have not come prepared.*

He would not let that stop him.

Delicious licks of cloudy heat poured from his body as he focused hard on the spot where the female was just beyond.

Vedikus lowered his axe back into its sheath and took a step back, looking for a means, or a small opening where he could lure her close enough to grab. *I cannot deny the needs of my clan.* Not with such an obscurely lucky opportunity.

One finger, one strand of hair on my side and I can pull her through the thick brush.

"Who's there!?" A new voice filled the space.

Vedikus froze, his hand dropping back to his axe's handle. The thick corded muscles of his arms rippled, ready for another bout of battle. He swiveled to locate the direction where the voice had come from but he did not sense another goblin or creature nearby, only the female's presence and the sounds of crushed leaves and twigs breaking.

"I heard you, lass! Come out now or pay the price!"

It's coming from the human world. He moved back toward the wall and pressed as close to her as possible. Sharp, excruciating waves of pain attacked him and the hedge sprouted thorns to stab through his exposed skin, filling him with viler poison.

I need to grab her. Now! He couldn't lose her, not after the moon had handed him this opportunity. He would not go back to his brothers without her after she had been offered. It would be too cruel. The shame... consuming.

The female's fear finally reached his nose and he realized he did not like the smell of it as much as he thought he would. Vedikus grimaced and strained his hand outward through the thick vines and even thicker magic. *She's right there!* A little more and he could tear her through.

This new man could not have her.

Try as he might, he couldn't pierce it. He drew his hand back, so filled with rage—resentment for the intruder —that he did the one thing he didn't want to do.

"If you do not want to be caught, female, then I suggest you run," he growled, warning her away. Vedikus fought his instincts. "Run!"

A series of noises filled his ears as his words took effect.

Vedikus dropped his hands onto his weapons, clenching their handles as he listened to her flee, listened to the man pursue her. His prick was hard and in the process of lubricating itself for an impossibility. A chase and catch he had no part of.

The female fled from him, from another, and was in danger in the one place he could not go after her. He slammed his fist into the hedge wall and was shot away. Burning magic filled his veins. Hatred coursed with it, spreading through his body, urging him to berserk, urging him to roar and give his location away. But he kept his mouth shut and listened to whatever he could on the other side until no sound came at all.

Minutes went by. Steam trailed out not only from his nose but also his mouth to release the buildup inside. When his body cooled, only determination remained.

His opportunity had passed but there would be another.

If she's caught... Vedikus hated the idea of anyone other

than himself giving chase, but if she *was* caught, she'd become a sacrifice. Hope alighted his blood.

He waited another few minutes, keeping his ears to the barrier, but there was no sound other than the wilderness to be heard.

The shrouded moon was full overhead and her smell was gone before he left the small glen behind, heading in the direction of the nearest sacrificial juncture: Thetras.

It would be crawling with barrier lurkers but he was ready to spill blood. If the female was to be thrown to the monsters, to him, it would be there.

He hated hope, had never believed a warrior should have it because a warrior should either know his outcome and believe in it, or fail; but as he quietly crept toward his destination, the slimy emotion whittled through his skull. Hope was an enchantment as lucrative and lying as the sun in his world.

I won't let the Bathyr down.

Anticipation fueled him.

Chapter Three

Tiny rivulets of blood leaked from her wrists and down the backs of her hands. It didn't stop her from pulling at the rope that bound them, though. She had no other option if she wanted a future. A little pain now could save her a lot of pain later.

Aldora dragged her feet as the Laslite hauled her by her arm. They stopped briefly at the spot where she had been discovered and picked up her bag.

Silence was heavy between them as he tied her to a branch and crouched to shuffle through her stuff. A couple of her mother's apples spilled out and onto the ground.

A bruised apple was a bad apple according to her parents, and it saddened her to see them handled so poorly.

It wasn't her privacy being invaded that kept her lips shut, but the possibility that the beast might still be there, waiting, listening; that he would speak again and damn her so completely that she'd have no recourse to talk her way out of this nightmare. Because that was what this was: a nightmare. One she and every other citizen of Savadon had at some point growing into adulthood. Savadon didn't build dungeons to house criminals. Savadon had a maze.

The monster didn't speak again and she was at once grateful and wistful. Despite her circumstances, her curiosity was piqued, and a beaconing tendril of dark adventure tempted her. Aldora wanted to hear the beast's voice again, wanted to feel its deep tonal heat enthrall her. The rumbling cadence of its words penetrated all the way to her bones.

It was wrong—deceptive—but achingly haunting. All she had were stories and a scattering of illustrations of what lay beyond the misty wall, and she wanted *more*.

He spoke my tongue. Her eyes narrowed to look at the looming treeline and vines, cast in monotonous shades of shadow and darkness. *How did he know my language if he isn't human? If all humans died crossing the barrier?* She ducked her head to rub it along her shoulder, removing the tangled hair from her face.

Not all humans died, Aldora corrected herself. Some made it back out alive. However, those that did were tainted and shunned by society. They were banished to the worst parts of Savadon, the deep swamps, the craggy shores, the mines. That's if they didn't go back into the mists. She'd never seen one of these survivors but was told she would know it if she did.

They came back marked.

The Laslite hefted her satchel over his shoulder with a snort of disgust and untied her from the tree.

"You must have offered up your demonic wares, your

bat wings, and will-o-wisps, before I caught you, witch," he spat. Spittle hit her collarbone and dribbled down into her tunic. "It matters not, the masters will see through you." He threw her forward and back onto the path. Her knees hit the ground and she cringed from the blunt impact. A moment later she was hauled back to her feet.

"I'm not a witch," she tried to say calmly but it came out shallow and shaky. Her fear hadn't abated, if anything, it had gotten worse. Sweat beaded her brow and under her arms. It mattered not that the night air was chilly, she felt nothing but anxious waves of heat.

"Lies, pretty peasant." They headed for the lights.

"I'm not…"

"You were speaking to something in the labyrinth. Only witches commune with the darkness and dirty freeman that can't tell a horse from a rock. Either way, Savadon, the last bastion of humanity, has no use for either. If you were smart, you should have wed and stayed out of sight. You know what happens to the idiots of the kingdom?"

Aldora remained silent.

"They're gotten rid of. Or…" The man stopped to look at her from head to toe, taking a moment to encroach her space and palm her breast. "Or pretty ones like you spread their thighs and learn to like it."

She tried to wrench back but his hold on her tightened. She buckled and screeched, kicking her legs back in hopes of landing a blow to his knees but the thick leather of his boots shielded it all. The Laslite chuckled and wrested her around to hold her from behind, his armored chest pressed heavy against her back. He groped her harder, keeping her in place with one arm banded around her midsection while moving his other down to cup her sex.

She froze from shock until he pressed his erection into her back. Aldora wrenched away from him and he let her go. She didn't even make it a yard before the Laslite took hold of her again and continued walking, a jolly, whistled tune on his lips.

If he was trying to break whatever last threads of courage she had left, he was doing a good job of it. The pinch of his grip on her arm made her sick with apprehension, but try as she might, the rope binding her wrists remained excruciatingly tight.

It wasn't until they came upon the first house that she realized they were in Thetras. The lanterns lighted the path far sooner than she would've liked.

Her gaze darted everywhere at once, hopeful in finding a friend, or someone who did business with her family. They would come to her defense—she hoped. It would be nothing but the power-hungry Laslite's word against hers. The Laslite didn't live here, they traveled the kingdom, watchful wanderers, and judges that spoke on behalf of the capital. The odds were against her, but it didn't stop her from hoping.

It was only those who had become "true sacrifices" that no one stood up for.

It was late at night, and no one she knew was out at this time. Those they passed only looked upon her with open curiosity. The same kind of curiosity that led her into this predicament to begin with.

Aldora sensed them following.

"Almost there, witch," the Laslite said.

She knew. She heard the commotion emanating from the tavern long before it came into sight. Shadowy figures meandered in the alleyways leading up to it, shady dealings, whispered arguments, and the grunts of bad sex met them before the rough, carved doors she knew so well.

Aldora had no idea what would happen once they crossed the threshold. She locked her legs and twisted toward her captor. "I'm not a witch," she begged. "You don't have to do this. You know there's no proof. I've lived here my whole life and many in this town know me, they know my family, know how hardworking and law-abiding we are. I am!" She raised her head and met the Laslite's eyes, seeing them clearly for the first time. "I'll do anything," she finished on a whisper. She would if it meant all of this would go away.

If she could be back in her family's fields tomorrow, with no one the wiser but herself about what had happened, she would do *anything*.

Her resolve turned to stone as she stared at the patroller. Aldora knew she couldn't get away from him. The bindings on her wrists were too strong, and even if she did manage to escape, fleeing back into the forest and slipping away, she'd still be bound, leaving a trail of blood for the wolves.

Were she to make it safely home and remove the bindings, she wouldn't be able to stay.

I could do it, I could survive. For how long, though? She was a farmer, not a hunter nor a soldier. She was better at planning than she was at fighting and she knew it.

But I am a hider.

My body is strong. I can endure... Her eyes shifted away from the Laslite.

I can pretend.

"Pretty words but not pretty enough for me, witch. Do you want to know something? A secret perhaps?" The tavern doors knocked open and a laughing couple poured out and walked by without a glance. The lute playing within grew louder. He dragged her inside and leaned toward her ear. "During our final year of training to become a Laslite, witches are set upon us throughout that time to test us, witches enslaved by the king. That shocks you doesn't it?" He didn't give her a chance to respond. "They could come upon us at any time, anywhere, whether it was during field training or in the middle of the night, whether it was a whore at the tavern just like this, or a servant taking away your plate. We had to stay vigilant, watchful, but we could not assume. To assume was to be paranoid, and a paranoid Laslite was worthless. But each witch had something in common, something only a Laslite could recognize, and why nothing you say could ever change that. Do you want to know what it is?"

Aldora shuddered and nodded, peering at him nervously through the candlelight. She shouldn't care what her captor had to say but she wanted to know, wanted to know what damned her so entirely in his eyes.

"You all smell of fruit."

Aldora narrowed her eyes and her brow furrowed. *Apples.* He turned on his heel and tugged her toward the door.

"But I work in an orchard," she argued, wrenching back. "You saw the apples in my bag."

He *humphed* and they were suddenly surrounded by sticky mead and honey music. "I heard you talking to something beyond the barrier." His words were drowned out by the sudden uproar of laughter and cups being slammed and shuffled on tables. Everyone looked up and tracked them with their gazes as they passed. She heard the tavern door opening and closing several times as those who had followed them from town entered the establishment. Some of the noise dulled as she was hauled toward the back of the room, wincing as chairs and table corners banged into her sides.

With sudden violence, and before she could fight him off, her captor picked her up and threw her across the table. She landed on top of the steaming bowls of soup and goblets of liquor, directly in front of the glazed-eyed Master of Thetras, Nithers Emen.

"I've found the reason why the mists are seeping," the Laslite declared.

A sickening hush fell across the room.

Aldora gasped and cried out, flinching away from the metal and scalding liquid that soaked into her clothes. Her arms wiggled under her, crushed and battered by the sudden force of being thrown. She lifted her head and whimpered, feeling a sharp stab of pain where it had slammed into an iron cup.

"What is the meaning of this?" Nithers demanded.

Hands were on her the next moment, dragging her off the table and forcing her to stand, and it took all her strength to stay upright despite being held up by her arm. Hot and cold liquid streamed down her body to pool inside and around her boots.

"This," she recognized her captor's voice, "is a witch. One I came across speaking to something beyond the barrier."

"Aldora? Aldora is a witch?"

At her name, she looked up at Master Nithers. He had a town's lady cooing on his lap and his hands were fondling her bared breasts. Aldora recognized the girl as the blacksmith's daughter, Hypathia, and immediately understood. She was an innocent who, like most budding females along the bordertowns, was in the process of losing it.

All the women of Thetras, and she assumed all other bordertowns, understood. To be pure, virginal, was to make a great sacrifice. Aldora had never understood why. Her bitterness had led her to believe that men found women who were untouched by other men worthy of something more—like death. *If we cannot be touched then there is nothing stopping us from being killed.* Aldora had done the same thing, in this very tavern, several years back. The tavern whores always knew the best men to send a maiden to.

Hypathia was disinterested, her features neutral, her body unresponsive. Her nipples weren't even puckered. But to go to the Master for an introduction? He either paid a whore a large amount of coin, or Hypathia was seeking safety beyond her standing.

"Aldora's not a witch," Hypathia offered meekly. A weak defense but enough to give Aldora hope.

Pretend. She lowered her head subserviently to peer through her lashes. She wasn't a witch but she also wasn't a simpering innocent. "This is all a mistake, my lord."

"I found her next to the wall after sundown, speaking

to something, some creature, maybe even the mist itself without pretense," the Laslite said.

"That's not true!" she pleaded, and a shiver shot through her remembering the dark voice. "It was a misunderstanding. I heard children and wanted to make sure they were safe. You know they play dangerous games." Aldora hoped it was enough to convince Nithers. She hated lying, but her options left little recourse.

"Quiet! Both of you!" Nithers squinted at her and then the Laslite. "When did this all happen?"

Hushed conversations filled the tavern; without looking, she knew they were all about her.

"Not an hour ago, my lord."

"Where?"

Both Aldora and the Laslite answered at once.

"—Between Thetras and Ledger—" she blurted.

"—Outside of town, on the world path leading to Nestras—"

The Laslite's grip tightened on her arm. Pain shot through her and she bent over, praying someone would step in and save her. "He assaulted me," she whimpered.

"Don't listen to her lies." The Laslite hit the table with his fist. "She spoke of tricks and is manipulating you now. I have encountered many witches in my travels and I guarantee, on the king's honor, that she is one!"

Others in the tavern started to speak up, spewing their own opinions that she could neither argue nor agree with. Tears slid down her cheeks and settled on her lips, her chin, where they eventually fell from her face.

"The mists have gotten worse, it started years ago," someone said.

"Burlox fell less than a fortnight ago! We're not safe."
Another voice, louder, and more frantic.

"We're all in danger! Look at her! If she'd been
assaulted, she'd have more than mead and stew marring
her."

Nithers shoved Hypathia off him and stood. She fell to
the floor and quickly covered herself before she scrambled
away, her eyes alight with fear and pity. *For me.* Nithers
leaned across the table and scanned Aldora from head
to foot.

"You can see, Master of Thetras, that she is a liar," the
Laslite said smugly.

Nithers waved his hand and the room descended back
into silence. He opened his mouth and a moist breath that
reeked of mead blasted her face. She flinched away.

"A-Aldora," he slurred. "I do not know you well but
answer me this question."

She stilled, unsure of what he would ask of her.

"Whose children did you hear out there so late in the
twilight?"

Aldora paused, confused before realizing he meant her
story. Tears slid down her face. She didn't have an answer
because to answer was to incriminate and she couldn't do
that to an innocent. Could never to that. Not even to save
herself.

Her silence was damning enough.

"Sacrifice her to the mists!" A yell went out that was
quickly picked up by others. It grew until it drowned her,
solidifying her fate.

She thought she would—could—do anything to end
this nightmare. She'd been wrong.

Chapter Four

Vedikus heard the chanting of humans long before he made it into position. He gritted his teeth as he dropped his stealth and headed toward the noise. He'd been waiting in the shadows for the moon to slip directly overhead and into middling night, not long at all, and not even long enough to fully scout the perimeter and see what he was up against.

Thetras's sacrificial clearing reeked of hungry beasts. It was one of the only places that remained a free-for-all for human sacrifices. Other locations, some far, some near, were ruled by different tribes and monsters. To capture a sacrifice within lich lands was near impossible.

His own hands were coated in blood from stealth attacks he'd performed from the shadows. The cursed mist dined upon them as he sprinted forward. The noise the humans made called others just like him to the location. In the distance he felt the thunderous strike of centaurs approaching, he heard the high-pitched shrieks of hobgoblins, and to his dismay, the sudden beat of an orc drum.

Vedikus unsheathed his axes, readying... His eyes sharpened as he entered the clearing.

A hobgoblin rushed in from across the way but was dead and twitching on the ground with an axe embedded in its head the next second. Vedikus stomped over and pulled his weapon from the body.

Two more came from his right and he sent his axe flying again. The one still standing hesitated long enough for him to pick up the corpse at his hooves and throw it, knocking the fleeing hobgoblin down under its weight. He walked over to the goblin's struggling form and hacked its head off before picking his other axe back up.

Vedikus swiveled around, ready for the next death.

A group of centaurs came next, the smell of their horseshit contaminating his nostrils when suddenly, he heard a human female scream.

"Please. Please, listen, I didn't do anything wrong! Please!" Her begging cries filled his ears and his eyesight sharpened further.

"Toss the witch cunt!"

"We will not be the next Burlox!"

A mob of noise built into a crescendo, breaking his focus. *I would kill them all if given the chance.* Vedikus glanced at the tiny silver orb of the moon and asked allowance to do so knowing it would never be given.

"Please at least let me say goodbye to my family!" the female cried. And for some reason it enraged him.

Vedikus's lips parted and heat suffused his face. The centaurs watched him as they spread into an arch on either side of him, their spears all loosely poised in their hands.

"Minotaur, we would rather not fight you," the middle one said. His hoof lifted and stamped the ground, breaking bones from long ago battles beneath it. "Our peoples are not enemies. Do not cause this to change."

Vedikus gripped his axes. "Not when it comes to this."

The centaur's lip twitched, revealing a chipped tooth. His hair was long and braided, broken knots and messy but adorned with wooden beads and shells. *A stud by the sea.*

"No." The centaur nodded. "Not when it comes to this, but still, we find you in our way."

"Then you must go through me for the female."

The centaurs growled in unison, and three sets of bloodthirsty, amber eyes trained on him.

"You know the sacrifice is female?" the one on the left asked.

"Can't you hear her screams?" Vedikus fumed, letting his horns dip in warning. "I've spoken to her. She is already mine." Her cries were at his back, and the sound of the pulley on the other side of the barrier sounded with a screech. The thrill and excitement of her people's jeers bolstered with each piercing turn. With it deepened the approaching drums of the orcs. His eyes stayed on the stallions. He still had time to kill them.

They swiveled toward the sound and readied for the coming attack. Orcs were a nasty business.

Vedikus stepped back toward the wall he now guarded. He prepared to protect what advantage he had. They would not take his spot over his gushing dead husk.

"You've spoken to this female? How? Is she magiked?"

It was the left centaur again. His gaze darted around as he spoke. "Minos don't deal in witches."

"The Bathyr deal with no one," Vedikus taunted.

The stallion sneered and broke rank.

The middle horse, and what he presumed was the leader, lifted his hand.

"Stop Telner, I did not give the order to attack." The leader looked to Vedikus. "If it is as you say, will she choose you?"

She does not have a choice. "Yes. Only the vicious best capture the blood breeders. You against me? She would have no option but to choose me. I'm the safest bet. One look at your bulbous, hanging pricks and she'll choose a pack of nipping hobgoblins over you."

All three centaurs stomped their hooves and brayed angrily, not taking his mockery lightly. But it was true. Centaurs weren't rapists, but they were widely known for having a hard time with the humans they collected. They'd been known to resort to taking many measures to convince their human captives to bear their young. He found it weak that the species couldn't master them.

Telner moved closer and stood up on his back legs before bringing his front hooves down. The strewn-about bones and bone dust cracked and powdered the air. "You want a painful drawn-out death, minotaur, I'll give you one!"

Vedikus hoisted his axes and positioned his legs, bowing his head slightly forward to jut his horns. The sound of the pulley had stopped and the pleas of the female were now almost directly overhead, high up in the mist and beyond anyone's sight. There wasn't much time before she fell. If the centaurs attacked him, he would only have moments to slay them.

"She's at the top!" the lead centaur yelled, lowering his spear. His men looked up just as the orcs entered the clearing. They hesitated.

Vedikus slammed his axes into the ground and used it to his advantage. "Protect me while I catch her!"

The sacrifice had come all too quickly and that hope he had felt earlier had stabbed him in the back. If there'd been more time, he wouldn't need any beast's help. But he had to catch her fall. He could not chance her life.

Vedikus didn't wait to see what the stallions chose to do, but when their spears didn't pierce his back and the battle cries of the orcs sounded, he assumed they shielded him.

"You will let her choose, Minotaur! Or face the consequences," the centaur leader shouted in warning.

Vedikus grunted but his focus was on the mist above him—its thick impenetrable shroud—as he watched for her fall. He bent his knees and lifted his arms, readying for the exact moment to catch her. His jaw tightened at the thought of her landing on his horns or crashing into the bone-strewn dirt.

"We give this sacrifice willingly to the labyrinth… To honor the magic that protects us from those trapped within… May this human feed your hunger and deliver us safety from your wrath and your expansion…" A haunting, jeering chorus of voices droned out the rites. The female had gone eerily quiet. It wasn't that he couldn't hear her amongst the ruckus but that she'd likely given up trying to persuade her people.

Cretins.

Fear—both monstrous and human—mixed with the blood of his enemies behind him threatened to drown his senses. Vedikus crushed his tongue between his teeth, flicking his eyes back and forth. Watchful. Angry.

Waiting.

He had her. He just needed to catch her first.

"This life for ours… For those who bask in the sunlight and live in humanity's kingdom remain forever guarded against magic and curse."

The chanting stopped and the humans went silent.

The battle shrieks behind him intensified. More had joined the fray. Vedikus felt the ravenous chaos building around him. He knew all of it wasn't for the human, but for its fresh blood. Human blood meant everything. Vedikus released the heat from his chest with a growl. This human was his. Blood and all.

A cascade of applause and cheers filled the mist.

Vedikus tensed, anticipating the moment the female appeared.

Where? He searched the darkness above him. The roars of the battle happening behind him grew closer.

Her frightened whimper came first, followed by a fluttering of cloth in the breeze, then a flailing form appeared. A howl went up behind him and Vedikus pivoted to the right, reaching…

He caught her, crouching down to cushion as much of her landing as possible.

Vedikus stared down at the female. Her eyes were clenched shut, her body tensed harder than petrified wood, and she had long dark hair, half-braided but mostly tangled around her face. *She's wet.* He gripped her tighter to his chest, careful not to press her against the weapons still buckled to him.

His blood-slickened, sweaty hands pressed into her skin and he felt her pulse race beneath his fingers. Though the mists began to clear around them, her features remained unformed in the dark. There were no glimmers or firebeetles to light her face for his perusal, but he knew when she opened her eyes to look up at him.

His muscles strained and his body began to prepare itself...

A shriek at his back had him swiveling on his hooves, grasping the handle of his axe, and swinging it with devastating efficacy at whatever dared to approach him. Vedikus kept the female trapped to his side as he watched the blade of his weapon sink deep into an orc's shoulder. Blood gushed out as its sword clattered to the ground. He yanked his axe out and let his opponent drop.

More creatures entered the fray, frenzied by the scent of her blood. They began to overwhelm the centaurs. His gaze darted past them as he looked for an escape. The female shoved against him.

"Stop!" he ordered.

Her fighting struggles only increased.

Vedikus flicked the excess blood off his weapon and pushed her back up against the labyrinth wall. A heavy, alarmed gasp escaped her lips and he leaned over her, shielding her from the slaughter.

"You know me," he hissed, giving her no opportunity to look anywhere else. "You know me," Vedikus said again. He didn't know why he cared.

"You…" she wheezed and slunk away from him.

"Do you want to live?" he asked carefully, his voice hoarse. His free hand cupped the back of her neck.

She answered with another whimper.

"Well?" he asked again. The female shook under his palm. The shock of the fall was leaving her system. Vedikus didn't want to let her go. The feel of her hair on the back of his hand did something to him and he felt his blood quickened. But not for battle... The female nodded and he grunted. "Then do not move from this spot. Do not *move*."

Vedikus squeezed her nape then let her go, watching her. When she didn't immediately flee, and with one eye still on her prostrated form, he nudged the shortsword the orc had dropped toward her feet. The haze of battle was already taking over and clouding his mind. He would touch her again when everything was dead.

Without another look, he picked up his other battle axe and turned to face the maelstrom.

———

I'm alive.

Her skin burned where the creature had touched her. Her pulse strummed wildly under her skin. She wanted to make it stop, to rub the feel of it off, but her hands remained bound with rope.

In a sudden rabid effort she wrested and fought to break free but the rope held strong and only tore her skin further. She kept trying despite the pain, unable to allow herself to stop.

Stopping meant death.

I'm not dead yet.

Aldora searched for an escape or a safer hiding place. Her eyes found her catcher though, and each time she looked away, they drifted back.

The large, hunkering shadow of him filled her vision. If it wasn't an illusion within the midnight gloom, the beast had horns jutting from the sides of its head. It was the only true feature she could make out. The rest, including the chaos behind him, were all just a bunch of blurry shapes.

But she knew him. The moment he spoke and his darkly cadent voice sounded—drowning out everything else—Aldora knew it was *him*. He was the reason she was here.

She shuffled to the side, deeper into the vines. Something scraped her boot. She dropped her gaze to see what it was, recalling that he had kicked something toward her.

Aldora slipped down the hedge wall. *A weapon. Oh light, a blade?* She turned to her side and extended her searching hands out behind her. Her fingers touched lukewarm metal. She grabbed the sword handle and tugged it further into the vines. Its weight was too much for her to wield in her current position.

Her attention shifted to the battle before her and the hissing, screeching roars of what she could not make out. *I- I don't want to know.* She struggled to lift the sword upright against the wall. Shapes of horses drew her hurried gaze.

Not horses. Centaurs.

She grasped the weapon tighter, her hands wet with sweat, and managed to wedge the crossguard into the ground and expose the edge of the blade. *Freedom!* Furiously, she slid her bindings against it, and with each snap of a cord, her speed increased.

Aldora worked feverishly while watching the frenzy, learning whatever she could while she was still immobilized. Spinely creatures, large brutish, humanoid beings, and other things she could not fully make out flitted throughout, moving in then retreating, or perishing in their attempts. What she couldn't see, she could smell.

And it smelled like death.

There were thick tree trunks and walls on every side of her, and Aldora realized she was in an open space. A clearing of sorts and unlike what she expected of the labyrinth, of what the stories had said. She'd thought the other side would be endless walls and trees.

She angled her head up but already knew she would never be able to climb the barrier wall to safety.

Another snap of rope loosened her joined wrists an inch. Her heart was in her throat, strangling her from the inside.

She glanced back to her horned catcher and the bodies that continuously fell at his feet. Shapes came at him from all sides, small and large to attack him at once, but each fell like her rag-dollies to the ground.

The violence of her catcher kept drawing her back, just like his voice had earlier. Large arms, thicker than humanly possible, jutted from his sides to hold a weapon in each hand, elongating his shadowy limbs in twisted and distorted ways. He swept them in arcs, spinning and swiveling, hacking and slicing straight through whatever came near.

Aldora felt his power and his violence, could almost

taste its potency on her tongue. The more enemies that fell at his hand, the faster and more brutal he became. As if each kill fueled his bloodlust further.

She drew back into the foliage and tried to breathe.

He's shielding me.

Nothing got past him. No matter how many beings tried, even those that attempted to dodge his attacks and sneak past him were stopped with blunt ferocity. The air quickened about her ears. Her matted hair rose and fluttered about. Each moment the charge coming from him grew. The shadows began to mold into one.

Aldora leaned forward, drawn to the energy. Until it was broken by a voice.

"Elscalien, Telner, on the offense, drive them back!"

She'd ceased moving her wrists and in renewed hurry, Aldora pressed the rope harder against the blade's edge. Moments later her wrists fell away and were finally free. She shook them once but knew she couldn't stop moving, and despite the pain, she reached back and grasped the handle of the shortsword and brandished it, rising to her feet.

I'm not a warrior but a hider. She looked around to do what she was good at before making a move. Common sense trumped ability.

Her eyes returned to him where he fought off a swarm of short, gangly creatures. *I need to get around him.*

He'd kept her from harm but for how long? She'd trust him to keep her safe until the end of the fight, but it was what happened after that worried her.

There was little opening but she spied several pathways where creatures gathered, pouring into the clearing. But one was quiet and Aldora focused on it. If she was going to hide—to run—it had to be now, before the monsters remembered she was there.

Before *he* returned to claim his prize.

What will he do to me?

Would he rape her? Or worse, feast on her flesh as he did so? Her mind raced with horrid possibilities. She wiped her tears on the back of her hand.

I can't stay here. Her heart threatened to explode.

Without waiting for a better chance, she pressed back into the hedge wall and made her way along it, under the creeping vines, and toward the only clear path in sight.

She came upon a rotting tree midway—and with a quick glance back at the horned beast to make sure he wasn't searching for her—she moved toward it, running her body along the tree's side until she faced the open path. Aldora counted to five, peering through the gloom to see if anything would jump out of it, or dash in. But nothing did.

Go. She twitched.

Aldora took a steadying breath and lowered her sword, and with a quick swipe of her sleeve across her forehead she—

"Female!" Pure rage vibrated the air. "Where is she!?"

She fled into the labyrinth.

Chapter Five

Vedikus stormed away from where the female had been, filled with fury. He spotted a shape dart into the darkness to his right.

"Minotaur! You lost her!?" The chief centaur screamed, kicking his legs back. Several goblins shot across the clearing. Vedikus ignored him and ran after the girl. He was out of the sacrificial zone and at the first fork within moments, without another glimpse of her.

Where is she? There were bodies strewn about but none of them were hers. *Right or left?* Vedikus swayed his head back and forth, releasing steam. *Which way?*

Telner appeared suddenly out of the darkness from his left, galloping toward him and flicking blood off his spear.

Not left.

"Where are you going, bull? Where's the female?" Concerned, agitated anger spurted from the stallion. "I'll kill you for this!"

Telner charged him.

Vedikus had no time for horseshit and sprinted down the right-hand path. It soon forked again and he halted.

I can't lose her. His victory meant nothing without a celebration with his prize. He regretted offering her a blade.

Two options, but as he searched both paths, Telner reappeared. Vedikus growled at him in warning. His vision blurred. Minutes ago he'd barely held himself back from going berserk and the need to do so only increased. He cursed the female.

If he and his brothers hadn't needed her so badly, picking a direction would be easy.

He chose the right-hand path again. Immediately after his skull cleared and he stopped.

She never came this way.

Vedikus looked up at the partially hidden moon and thanked her, turning on his hooves. *Maybe the female* is *a witch.*

His mother had been.

And if she had taught him anything, it was that humans were unpredictable, determined, and did unexpected things when scared or threatened.

"Minotaur!" Telner roared, closing in.

Vedikus faced the centaur and pulled out his axes.

"Failure assumes I have lost. I've lost nothing, horse, and to assume as much is to ask for death." His fingers adjusted on his weapon.

"Then where is she? Where's the female? We had a deal, and your kindred would be ashamed if you wronged my people. We are neutral!" Telner rose up on his hind legs and crashed back down. The ground trembled between them.

"She's hiding." Vedikus looked past him.

"Where? Produce her now. She must make a choice."

Over my cursed vile blood. He had never agreed. He used and discarded, and honed his endurance and strength without help. Vedikus and his brothers had a different way of accomplishing their goals, their own blood-code with the first Minotaur, and they walked alone because their way of thinking disagreed with the others of his people.

The Bathyr had left their mother tribe behind to traverse the labyrinth and begin anew. Not one bull followed them into the outer mists. And because he and his brothers had bound together, they became a brotherhood of warriors. His only regret about that day was that he was leaving innocents of his previous tribe unprotected. To lose their best warriors was the price his old tribe had paid for wronging them.

Because they *had* wronged the Bathyr and dishonored their mother. Even now her bones were missing, and his sire slept alone, waiting for his mate's return in his eternal slumber. Until her bones were restored and put properly to rest, the Bathyr would never return to the mother tribe.

Vedikus raised his axes and charged at the centaur.

The female is mine.

Telner reared up and aimed his spear to the ground as Vedikus angled his head down, positioning his horns. The power behind a minotaur charge was on par to none, and the centaur realized a moment too late that death was on the table.

He rammed head first into the stallion just as Telnar's two front hooves crashed down. He screamed and Vedikus felt the sharpened point of the centaur's spear slice deep across his back. He thrust his horns straight through Telner's leather armor and deep into the centaur's torso. Thick warm liquid burst over his head and down his face, splashing over his eyes and onto his lips.

Horseshit blood filled his mouth. He shook his head back and forth, ravaging the centaur's chest. The spear pierced his back several more times before it sunk in deep and stayed there. Telner's body slackened.

Vedikus gripped the centaur's front legs and hefted the heavy weight off him, sliding his horns free. More gore spilled over his body as Telner's twitching, weakly braying form dropped to the ground.

The centaur looked up at him. "You'll pay for this," he rasped.

Vedikus kneeled beside him. "I've already paid. More than you can ever know. Horseshit can't win against a minotaur alone. If you wanted to truly feed my blood to the mist, you would've waited for your brethren. You let your battle lust win and in doing so, will die a fool's death."

Telner curled his lips and sneered. "This won't kill me."

Vedikus looked at what was left of Telner's chest. He'd fatally punctured the stallion's lungs and intestines. It was only a matter of hours, possibly minutes before the stud died. No feelings of remorse coursed through him nor thoughts of regret.

Only the strong, the intelligent, survived the world

labyrinth, and a young centaur leaving his chief to battle a minotaur was neither.

Vedikus chanted his final rites and rose to his cloven feet. He stepped over the centaur's struggling body and backtracked toward the sacrificial zone. Telner's curses followed him until the mist devoured them like it did everything else.

Even now the mist licked at his rent back. The more carnage there was, the more it drew the hungering fog. But it was that same cursed brume that would bring him to his trophy.

He flicked his axes and sheathed them. Vedikus swiped the gore from his face. It was better on his hands where it couldn't blind him. Vedikus found the first fork and quickly disposed of several hobgoblins skittering throughout. He chose the left-hand path this time. His tail slapped against the leather loincloth at his back.

He looked up. *Daylight will be upon us soon.*

But he'd have the female long before then.

Aldora fled down the path, following the wall. She swiped vines away that reached for her and jumped over corpses. Heavy steps sounded right behind her.

She drew her sword to her chest and searched for a place to hide. Her breaths came out in spurts, and sweat poured down her body.

She knew almost nothing about what really dwelled within the labyrinth and Aldora wasn't sure if the stories she'd been told could be trusted; except for the monsters with teeth made for crushing bones.

Ghouls, beasts, ghosts, and goblins.

Her fingers clenched around her weapon. At least she had that.

Aldora dove back into the vines at her side and slipped in as far as the hedge would let her. She'd barely made it within before the beast was upon her. A thousand thorns pricked and sliced into her flesh on all sides, worse than those that had punctured her at the barrier. A whimper escaped her lips before she drew her hand up over them. The air was hot and heavy against her palm.

The shadow hovered, stilled and looked at the split trail like she had. The thing was massive, far more so standing so near, and Aldora was certain he toyed with her.

Please keep going. Don't hear my heart. She prayed.

Something slithered across her scalp, burrowing through her hair and a screech caught in her throat. It took all her willpower not to tear out of the brush and claw it off.

"Minotaur! You lost her?"

Aldora eased back as the speaker approached from the left path. Its form was blocked by the horned beast directly in front of her.

She did not want to draw his attention, did not want him to find her. He may have caught her and protected her from the other fiends, but she otherwise had no idea what he had in store for her. Only hours ago they had spoken with a wall between them and his voice—with its seductively dark cadence—had enthralled her enough to keep her in place.

What he planned to do with her—to her—now that he had won was something she refused to find out. The only people she trusted were her family. The thought of them filled her with sadness and she quickly pushed them from her mind.

I will see them again...

I have to try.

The beast shot away and the centaur went in chase of him. Her hand remained poised over her mouth until she could no longer hear them, and when nothing else appeared, she tore out of the clinging vines and dropped her weapon, streaking her fingers through her hair.

She writhed frantically, leaning over to dislodge the critter on her head and the feel of its many, tiny legs. It tried to scurry away but she caught it under her boots as she stamped it into the ground. Aldora didn't stop until nothing remained. The feel of it lingered on her raised flesh.

She picked up her shortsword and dashed to the left, sprinting a dozen yards down a veering path that led farther away from the barrier. It sloped sharply and brought her to a halt. The canopy had thickened to block whatever small amount of light shone from the moon, but she could still see the pile of small, broken bodies that were clearly *not* human below.

Their smell was sour and fresh. Aldora drew closer, an eye on her surroundings until the corpses were at her feet. One held a dagger stretched out in front of him and she snatched it up to slip into her boot. She pushed the body over, she found a bag attached to its belt. In it were items she couldn't see but she took it anyway.

Howls arose in the distance and she shot to her feet.

Barghests.

Aldora looked around once more but she remained alone. *It won't be for long even if everything nearby has been killed. I need to hide.* She glanced up at the canopy. She had no idea what awaited up there but she'd confront bugs over monsters any night.

She made quick work stashing her sword and finding a grouping of vines against the wall strong enough to hold her weight. As if barghests snapped at her heels, she climbed using the last of her rapidly diminishing energy. The hedge wall tapered at the top and she clenched her jaw, refusing to let it deter her. She hauled herself over it to find a shallow hollow. The foliage thickened and the vines were tangled in mass where it had collected within.

Aldora wasted no time as she crawled inside, forcing the mass to the sides and then in front of her to hide behind. She drew her legs to her chest.

The thorny vines twirled like slow-moving snakes around her frame and penetrated her flesh. She squeezed her eyes shut.

I'll endure it. Endure it. Just long enough until the horrible sounds go away. I've climbed trees my whole life, I can climb the wall.

I need to regroup, to wait, and hide until it's light out. She would head for the barrier then. *It's not far.* Aldora could almost see it through the moonlight and mist. She just needed time to think clearly and come up with a plan that wasn't fueled by desperation and fear before she made the journey over the tops of the hedges and tried for the other side. Try or die.

I can do this.

She hugged her legs tightly. Time passed in a haze as the vines tightened around her, leaving her skin raw with pain. Her thoughts clouded as her struggling pants softened, her body relaxed a little more with each minute, and she succumbed to the feel of bugs crawling over her skin.

Until something grabbed her foot and yanked her to the labyrinth ground.

Chapter Six

Vedikus pulled the female into his arms and gripped her to his chest, pressing his hand over her mouth. She thrashed against him, but her struggles were weak, disjointed. She groaned under his fingers and squirmed as he positioned her to the ground to subdue her. When he had her locked in place, he bent over to meet her wild gaze.

Wildcat. Angry and unthinking. Her eyes narrowed above his hand and he knew she recognized him. The disgust that filled them was only diminished with caution. The female resisted and kicked her legs and he moved to straddle them.

What am I going to do with her? Now that he had caught her, his next step eluded him. *Get us away from here.* Vedikus looked briefly at the walls on either side. He could see them more clearly, even in the darkness, than he had in years. And he had been on this world for more years than he could count. *It's unsafe here.*

It was because of her. His eyes moved back to the female trapped beneath him.

"Do you hear that?" he asked, leaning closer to her ear. She stilled for a moment and settled, her focus apparent. She was obeying him. He grasped her tighter. "Those are the sounds of approaching enemies, the beat of several orc drums. If you can hear them, then you're too close, but what you don't hear is far more terrifying." Vedikus pressed into her, his lips hovering above her ear, and he felt the blood of those he'd defeated drip off him and onto her flesh, christening her first night in the mist.

She had no idea how fortunate she was.

"What you don't hear are the barghests prowling closer, just down the path, or the goblins that await in the same vines you were in, the ghosts that will as likely kill you as they would possess you. A sacrifice happened here tonight and every creature within leagues will know by sunrise. Those who are addicted to human blood will hunt for you relentlessly. Some monsters never give up. I don't." He lifted up slightly. "Will you scream?"

The female shook her head and he removed his hand from her mouth. The soft pucker of her lips, hot and wet, was the last his palm felt before he rubbed it on his loincloth.

"Why are you doing this?" she choked out.

"To keep you alive."

He should get up, unpin her, and lead her from this place, but he couldn't yet bring himself to move. She was soft and pliant under his warrior-hewn body and cushioned him everywhere he pressed and touched. So easily breakable, so easily conquered, that it made him question his sanity. How was he going to get her back to the Bathyr alive?

When his sire caught his mother many years ago, he never told Vedikus or his other sons how he had done it, only that it was with unrelenting determination and insatiable need. His sire had been crazed with exerting his control and trained his spawn to be the same way, beating them until it reached the point of evil.

She peered up at him warily, her face now marred with the dirt and blood from his hand. "Alive for what?"

Vedikus clenched his fist, replacing the feel of her lips, and stood, but not before he grasped her and hauled her up with him. He held her upright as she found her footing. He knew how soft and weak human feet were.

"So you can be of use to me and my brothers…" Branches rustled down the path from which they had come, and he raised his hand to quiet the female. A crackle and thump were followed by a groan. Vedikus settled his hand over the handle of his axe. He stared into the darkness from whence it came and waited for the attack.

Seconds passed without another noise. He dropped his hand and looked back in her direction. "No more talking. We need to leave now before the others stop killing each other and start searching for you," he whispered.

She didn't respond. He couldn't see her face in the shadows but he couldn't afford to wait much longer and assuage his curiosity. He needed to know that she wouldn't run or scream or fight him every step of the way.

When he was about to throw her over his shoulder, she turned up her face, halting him.

Her hand grasped his arm, but he could not look away from her face in the filtered moonlight.

Why is she touching me? Vedikus narrowed his eyes.

"I want to return home," she breathed with every last sorrowfully wistful note she had. He recognized the vulnerability in her plea, and it made him want to be a hero for a single sun-glimpsed moment in time.

But heroes died. They were fools.

He would always choose a hungering, festering life over death. Death meant an end to glory.

The skin where she clutched his arm burned. Vedikus growled out a burst of steam and flung her hand away.

"You have no home now, female, but you have your life and it is now mine. It will be mine until you breathe your last breath, and you will remain mine even when your heart stops beating and your blood is no longer fresh. Because even in death, there's no escape, no rest, only survival. This world will take it all if the brutal don't take it first, as I've taken you." Steam escaped his lips as he pointed to the barrier that loomed like a poison cloud above the paths and rotting trees. "The hundred dead behind us will grow until the labyrinth is impassible, do you understand? If you approach those walls, you'll have to walk over those bodies... and if you fall before the top, you'll land within their moldering husks and they will have won."

The female's mouth parted and he grasped her neck. "Choose your words carefully."

"I don't want them to win," she said, straightening, jerking out of his hold. The sadness from before was now gone.

He waited a moment before accepting her answer; there was no time to read into her response. Already, he could feel the thickening of the air around them, drawing non-sentient and malicious beings closer. He had to get her away before every step became a battle.

"No," Vedikus laughed softly. "No one wants *them* to win."

He reached for the rope around his hips.

The numbness that had kept her going seeped out of her all at once. It was a difficult stab of reality. Aldora had seen her life pass before her eyes as she laid flat under the beast, as his musky, sweaty smell crashed into her nose, and his face hovered above her own. The heat of his body pressed against hers had nearly suffocated the life from her lungs.

Now, she was at the end of the rope he'd tied around her waist. She'd pulled at the cord, trying to release herself, had even taken her dagger and tried to cut it, but it wasn't like the bindings of her world. Her captor had simply chuckled at her efforts.

"It's made from the wheat grown by where I live and threaded with witch hair. You will not be free of it as you will not be free of me."

There was barely two feet of give between them and he kept it taut, tugging her forward with every step.

He trusted her as much as she trusted him. Not at all.

They walked for an indeterminate amount of time and she didn't bother keeping track. She attempted to briefly, but everything around her remained shrouded in darkness, and after she lost sight of the giant wall, she stopped trying. There was nothing but twisted growth and forked passageways with every step and nothing to keep her oriented to their whereabouts.

Aldora held onto the straps across the beast's back and used them as leverage to keep her moving. When her strength waned, she took advantage of his. There was no sound between them but the crunch of his feet to the ground. She knew better than to speak at a time like this. Not with her ears already filled with every sort of sound that meant monsters were nearby. Even now, the persistent thunder of drums lingered in the distance.

Her eyes drifted to the plumes of dust below, unable to make out what about her captor made him crush the dirt.

Did she want to know what held her? Her nails dug into his buckle. He'd taken her away from her only hope of escape but he had also kept her alive. Her instincts warred, and the more she stared at the moving outline of his horns, the more her uncertainty grew.

He's not an Orc. Her knowledge of orcs, if the stories had been correct, was that they were muscled, barbaric men with tusks and blunt features. They ate humans, like her, and their hunger for flesh was endless. *Orcs travel in groups.*

Aldora squeezed her eyes shut and let the shadow drag her forward a few steps.

He wasn't a hobgoblin. That much was apparent. He had killed many prior to her capture and more as he led her away. Their bodies were half her size and contorted in unusual ways.

They hid in the foliage—like he had said—and also

attacked in groups. They were also easily overpowered if isolated from their comrades. Any knowledge she learned now could save her life later.

But it was her captor's horns and his size that really made him stand out. He was obviously not a centaur or a barghest, and she had not seen another monster with horns since being pushed into the labyrinth, at least she had not glimpsed another in the gloom.

He stopped suddenly and she fell into his back. His wet and torn back. Aldora leapt away.

He placed his hand over the weapon hanging from his side and she sucked in a breath, waiting for another attack. She took a half-step closer to him, her own hands poised on his back, and braced her feet apart in case she needed to move quickly. Minutes went by and nothing happened.

She strained to hear what he sensed.

Nothing. Nothing but the creeping, gruff night noises that had yet to stop. She pressed her lips together. His muscles moved under her palms.

The smell of his flesh refilled her nostrils, accompanied by the thick scent of iron and melted metal that reminded her of the blacksmith's shop. Aldora sucked it in, so thick it left a residue that she knew would remain for hours. It wasn't unpleasant—except for the blood—but it was cloying, and the longer she breathed it in, the more it seemed like it was taking away her own smell, eating it up and overpowering it.

She rubbed her nose.

He turned toward her and loosened the leash that bound her, allowing the rope to droop between them.

Aldora lifted her gaze to his face while still rubbing her nose.

"We're being followed," he said loud enough for only her to hear.

She licked her dry lips. "Is that...bad for me or for you?"

"Bad? No, more an annoyance, but would you risk another at this witching hour?"

Aldora wasn't sure if she would. "I don't know," she said behind her hands. She still could not smell herself.

"You don't want to know."

"No, I don't want to know. I want to go home," she agreed, turning her head to the side. "I don't want to know you or anything else about this place. I'm not supposed to be here."

"And yet, here you are, already losing your sense of smell."

She flinched and looked back at him. "How do you know?"

"It happens to all humans after breathing in the curse. Your blood is already tainting. We must keep moving."

His words filled her with dread. When the mist spread into Savadon's lands, all was lost within them. It would consume all that it touches and change it, twist it, make it into something new and unnatural. Was she going to lose herself too? It hadn't occurred to her until now that there could be more to its spread, that there could be dominion.

The beast turned its back to her and pulled on the rope, tugging her whole body forward. Aldora was forced to drop her hands to his belted cord and follow.

"I don't understand. What's happening to me?"

"You're adapting, degrading, and fast. Soon, your blood will be as corrupted as mine. Given a month's time, you'll be nothing more than a thrall."

"Can it be stopped?"

"Yes."

Aldora tightened her grip and tugged when he kept walking. "Will you stop it?"

"I don't have the right supplies on me." He continued to pull her along and she tripped after him. "But I will stop it."

His words gave her pause. She had expected a fight, had expected him to make her beg or worse, and for a few steps, she followed him meekly, wondering at his game. He had not hurt her, but he had lured her in with his voice, had not threatened her except with the unknown but had taken her far away from the barrier and kept her from returning home.

He was the only thing she smelled now.

Aldora stared at his back, resolving that she had no choice but to stay tied to his body.

They continued walking through the night, sometimes stopping to hide in hidden alcoves and brush, and her thoughts wavered between what was following them, and what was going to happen to her now. The land took a different shape and texture under her boots, becoming more sodden with each step. They passed piles of bones and fresh corpses, and the farther they traveled from Savadon, the denser the mist became. The creatures that she had seen hours prior had not re-appeared but she could still hear them.

When the darkness began to fade and a filmy, almost

burgundy and violet vapor lit the labyrinth around her, her endurance suddenly vanished. The wounds that had been inflicted upon her drained what was left inside, and she could still feel blood trickling from the backs of her wrists where the clots had reopened. Aldora could no longer pick her feet up, and she had given in to lean against her captor, pressing her cheek, sometimes her forehead to his spine. There was a line of hair that traveled it that tickled her nose.

She wasn't aware that she could see until he stopped and lifted her into his arms. It wasn't comfortable—his body was too hard—but she had no complaints; nothing left her mouth but a short gasp for fresh air as she found his face. Aldora inhaled.

Their eyes caught, but only briefly.

Her heart threatened to burst from her chest.

He was no longer a horned shadow but a flesh and blood being that appeared human, but not. His features were animalistic and blunted, as if he'd been born malformed, part beast, part man. Like a centaur but with features that blended rather than split right down the middle.

His ears stuck out under where his horns met his scalp, jutting out from the sides of his temple. They rose up slightly until they tapered into points. One flicked under her perusal.

He watched her as she studied him, too shocked to do anything else. If she cared for stealth it would've made her uneasy, but they were way beyond that now. Her booted feet swung with each of his tumultuous steps. No, the time for stealth had vanished with the dawn.

His forehead was large and wide to fit his horns and his nose swept down between two very human eyes. His nostrils flared and small puffs of steam released.

She'd felt it last night but now she knew where it came from. *His face.* Her insides squirmed. She was suddenly aware of how he clutched her to his chest.

Aldora tore her eyes from his face and moved to his shoulders, where their differences only grew. He had no real neck, or what there was of one was less defined. She blinked out the blurring in her eyes. It was either too thick and sinewed to be mistaken as part of his shoulders or his shoulders started from the back of his head and swept into a bulging, rippling cord of overlapping muscle.

What is he, if not a demon?

There was no way her hands would ever wrap around his throat, not that she would ever try. If she had to kill him, she'd go about it in a more effective manner. The straight, sharp edge of the dagger she had looted came to mind, solid within the side of her boot.

"Your eyes match your hair."

Aldora stiffened, thought his words over, and then nodded. "Yes."

His were black.

"Not all humans share the same features," he continued, his thick lips straightening. She waited for him to say more, but he didn't.

"No. We're all different," she whispered.

"Why?"

"I-I don't know. We get our looks from our parents and their lineage." She reached up to cup her neck, still stuck on his lack of one. "Both my parents have brown hair and eyes, so it would make sense for me to be born with brown hair and eyes."

"I've seen a human with blue eyes."

Another human? "You have? There are others alive, here in the labyrinth?"

He grunted. "Killing you is detrimental. There are others, but far away and far from us."

"And what about the one with blue eyes?" she asked, hopeful. "If you've seen them once, surely you can see them again. You killed countless last night…"

His nostrils flared for an instant then receded. "No."

Please. "No?" Her brow furrowed.

"They're dead," he snapped. Her gaze drifted back to his face.

"I'm sorry."

He snorted, and a sliver of sunlight pierced the mist to glint off one of his horns. "You're not sorry, and if you are, your sorrow is best deserved elsewhere. Those who were here before have nothing to do with you. If you want to survive in this place and to survive well, it's best to keep your emotions close." He looked away. "Nothing of mine can be weak."

Aldora lowered her eyes and rested her head against his iron-honed bicep. She would take his sentiment to heart.

Lost in her thoughts, it wasn't until they circled around a clearing for a second time before she realized they were off the winding paths. Her gaze lifted to a copse of trees so close together that they had tangled to become one long, strangely-shaped knot. The bark appeared wet, and as the beast walked past them for a third time, she discovered the wetness wasn't condensation but was coming from a seepage from within.

On the fourth pass, she squirmed and asked to be let down.

"I won't run," she breathed.

He stopped. "Won't you?"

Aldora grasped her wrist, biting down on her tongue.

"Tell me why."

She looked at the space around them, looked everywhere but at him and tried not to acknowledge that his hands had grown hot and damp where he touched her. "I won't run… because I don't want to die." She squeezed her wrist, uncomfortable, and afraid but not as afraid as before.

He walked them back to the trees and dropped her to her feet, making quick work of tying her to the warping branches. They twitched and moved at his touch, stretching to engulf the entity that disturbed them. She sat as far away as she could. They oozed over her rope.

He crouched a foot away from her, once again blocking her view of everything but him. His horns lifted up into the mist and an urge to grab them and twist them off overcame her.

"You don't want to die but there are more reasons to stay by my side. I want to hear them," he demanded.

Aldora pulled at her rope. "There are no other reasons, why would there be? You've taken all my chances away."

The beast snorted. "You spoke to me across the wall, female, if you can remember that far back. I did not answer you at first. I took none of your chances away."

"I thought you might've been a human trapped."

"And it was your sense of charity that stopped you? Are you charitable?"

Aldora narrowed her eyes. She'd given her mother's apples to the poor and the children of Thetras, had covered the work of those in need, had accepted her life as a peasant and a farmer, as a nobody who could not so much as force a flower to grow as make a change in the world. "I'm not charitable," she said after a minute, thinking of all that she could have done but hadn't. "I was curious, but I'm not a bad person. I've never hurt someone intentionally, and if you had been a trapped human, I would've helped."

"I was curious too," he said after a moment. "But I'm not charitable either, nor am I kind. I have no delusions of goodness, not here, not in this place. I have hurt beings intentionally and…"

She waited but he just stared at her. "And?" she asked softly.

"And if you run again, I will hunt you down, subdue you, tie you up and drag you naked and sobbing through these dangerous lands and watch whatever hope you have left wither, happily. There's a high cost for life, and one you will pay for."

He moved away and circled the clearing again. Her gaze dropped to settle on his inhuman feet. *No, not feet. Hooves.* She hugged her arms around her stomach, trying not to watch him, but her eyes would not leave his body.

The fear that the morning light had diminished had come roaring back to life. It further clawed at her insides as she realized how futile it would be to run. He was twice her size, if not more, and naked except for a thick loincloth that draped his front and back. It left nothing to her imagination, and every part of him that was human versus animal was fully on display for her.

He. It. Thing.

Aldora knew him for his maleness from the very core of her soul. It wasn't that he looked like a human male, it was the abysmal, unbreakable aura that threatened to drown her whenever he neared. They were alone, and being a female, she was worried.

He stopped in the middle of the clearing, barely an arm's length away, and grasped the ties hanging at his sides, removing them.

They landed on the murky ground with a *splat*.

"I won't run," she mustered warily. His head snapped up to peer at her. "I won't run because I want to live and…" she sucked in air through her nose, "I can't smell anything but you anymore." Aldora tore her eyes from him to look at the fog overhead. "I don't know where we are, and even if I made it back to the barrier, I'm in no state to make the climb." Her body was on the verge of collapse. "But…"

He made no move to speak and she clutched her arms tighter.

"I'm sad."

The silence that stretched between them had her curling up on her side on the wet ground. The quiet lingered far after he had risen to his feet and stormed off and out of her sight. It was the best gift he could've given her.

Aldora closed her eyes against where his form had long since vanished and wished she could smell the dirt beneath her cheek.

That she could smell anything that wasn't him, anything at all.

Chapter Seven

Noon light played upon the female's face, casting a multitude of weak colors over her soft features. They were more vibrant than anything he had seen in years and he relished the renewed hues.

His gaze drew back to her skin. It was darker than the pale flesh he knew of, as if it were kissed by the sun, and it shimmered like oil over hedge-bread. She did not have the sallow look that he thought all humans had but instead appeared healthy, as though she was forged by sunlight.

It won't last...

He stamped the memory of her as she appeared now because there would be no more sunlight left in her life with him, nor with the Bathyr.

Vedikus returned to the center of the copse and deposited the items he had foraged onto the tops of his bags. He pulled his axes from their sheaths and unstrapped his buckles, one by one, letting them hit the dirt. The bone knives, the herbs, his mementos he kept from battle all fell away from his body until it was just him, his cloth, and his wounds.

The gouges across his back had begun to fester and itch. There were more along his arms and legs, a bite mark above his ankle, and more still in random places upon his body. He looked at the sleeping female. She was in as much pain as him and he had prolonged it, knowingly, seeing how long her endurance would last.

Far longer than expected. He positioned several branches he had collected in a pile and breathed over them. They crackled and glowed like fading embers before igniting into fire, releasing tendrils of grey smoke to join the equally grey mist.

The air began to fill with the smell of fire. It would bring others to them, so he quickened his pace; there was nothing that made him more bloodthirsty than being interrupted.

Vedikus gave half his focus to the slumbering female on the ground, curious about her ability to sleep in such a dangerous place, while the other half listened for scouts. *Humans are weak.* A minotaur could go days without needing sleep.

I've convinced her she is safe with me. He snorted, straightened, and with his bone dagger now in hand, hacked a tangle of vines to bring back to the flames. Without a mortar and pestle, he crushed them with his hands until every last drop of dew was released. They filled his bone bowl almost halfway and he placed it atop the burning branches.

The smell that arose was cloying and rank.

He'd only been near one human in his life and his knowledge of them was limited. His mother had been cryptic and forgetful when telling her bull-sons her stories and his sire thought stories were for the weak. She'd had pale moonlight skin and wide glowing blue eyes, so unlike the female he captured. It was unexpected.

This female was larger than his mother, with a frame that tightened under his fingers. She appeared strong, even in sleep, and it eased a little bit of the urgency within him.

Vedikus opened one of his pouches and added wetwort, blimbery, and cove to his bowl. The concoction bubbled and turned a dull green. He stirred it with his finger, adding his own essence into the mix.

He hadn't been trying to capture a human when scouting the barrier paths, but he could not ignore a gift from the moon, not such a precious one, nor the opportunity she presented. She would breed with him and solidify the next generation of his clan, and having her among his brothers would tribalize them. No minotaur female had followed the Bathyr from the mother tribe.

Breed. His eyes trailed back to her prone figure. His body twitched. All human females caught and carried away were bred in some way in the mists. It was a better fate than being a blood bag for the feasters or a source of ingredients for liches and warlocks.

Vedikus stopped stirring and leaned forward, looking closer at her. *My brothers will want her, might fight me for her.* She was shapely and built and had that exotic skin coloring —that glow he was positive would taste like the sun. His tongue thickened and he swallowed a mouthful of thick saliva. *Hungry.* She was tied down and at his mercy. His bulbous member stiffened slowly under his leathers. He would not fight it or touch it, knowing the moment he did, it would distract him from all else. Even her.

I could fill her with my strength before the sky grows dark. The idea of watching her belly grow large, with her womb filled with bull, made his tail tap and slither across the backs of his thighs. He saw a glimpse of the future in his skull. Though to breed in such a dangerous place with both of them wounded would only get them killed.

But he considered it.

Her eyelids fluttered with dreams and Vedikus sat back. His taut stomach burned from leaning over the flames for too long. With a grunt, he scooped some of the paste from his bowl with his fingers and spread it over his skin. Within minutes the pain vanished.

First, he needed the tools to stop her corruption, then, he needed to deliver her to his brothers where she would have the extra protection to keep her safe.

Vedikus twisted his lips, feeling the pressure of his cock weaken. He hated that he needed the human to better the lives of the Bathyr with as much fervor as his member wanted to penetrate her. He grabbed the bone bowl and moved to her side.

She was a tool of the Bathyr now, and his personal burden.

What am I going to do with her? His wet fingers pressed into her exposed skin. If they survived the trek to the mountains, through Prayer, it would be a question he'd have to answer. If his mother were still alive…

He clenched his fists.

Vedikus released them and untied the rope at her waist. He grasped her hair and angled her head back. "Awaken."

Her eyelids flickered but did not open.

He lifted her in his arms and set her before the fire. She did not fight his hold, did not do anything at all but slip to the ground when he let her go. Vedikus pressed his mouth above her own and inhaled her breaths.

Weak, shallow, and twinged with a bitterness he could not attribute to blood. *Viler poisoning.* He tore off her boots and clothes, leaving them in dirty heaps at his sides until she was bare except for her underthings. Hundreds of tiny red dots and pink scratches revealed themselves from her cheeks to her shins. *Not once had she mentioned pain or faltered under her ailments.*

A hiss escaped his lips as his eyes found a large black bruise encasing one of her upper arms and the raw flesh on her wrists. All hidden under the long shredded sleeves of her tunic and pants.

Infuriated, Vedikus stormed to the vines and ripped off an armload to bring to her side. He squeezed the liquid out of them, splashing the excess over the female's bare skin. His tail lashed from side to side.

Her body startled upright like the newly undead and a shriek filled his ears. Vedikus placed his hand on the center of her chest and pressed her to the ground.

"Relax!" he rasped, her panic seeping into him. She only fought him more, clawing frantically under his weight. "Relax," he repeated louder.

"What's that feeling?" Her eyes widened, her nails

dragging at her skin. Confusion. "There's something inside me!"

Vedikus grasped her wrists with one hand and pinned her legs down with the other. The force of his actions was more violent than he intended but a couple more bruises were better than opening her wounds deeper.

"Female, do you remember the thorns?" he asked slowly, waiting for her struggles to subside. She stared at him for a time without blinking before she answered.

"Yes."

"They pricked you everywhere." He indicated her body and she raised her head to look.

"Yes." A barely-there breath.

"Some of them took root inside you."

She dropped her head back to the ground and silently cried. A black cloud of possession filled his gut and bloomed throughout his body. He wanted to lick over every prick on her flesh and reclaim it for his own, but he knew that doing so would not cure her.

It was still better than the alternative.

"This will hurt… What's your name?" he asked, voice hoarse.

"Aldora," she said between sobs, her limbs shaking under his. *She's under my grip*, he reminded himself. *Not tangled in rapist vines.*

"Aldora," Vedikus repeated, "hold still." He didn't wait for her response as he emptied out one of his pouches and stuffed it in her mouth. Her tear-filled eyes followed his every movement. He grasped the bone bowl and its boiling contents and poured the mixture across her skin, watching her flesh redden with heat. Her body spasmed, fighting it, her eyes squeezed shut as tears flowed freely down her face.

It wasn't until her body relaxed and he unpinned her legs that he realized he hadn't breathed since she'd given her name. He pulled the pouch from her mouth and brought the same bowl to her lips, tilting it for her to swallow its contents, knowing the slight euphoria of the cove would offset the scalding liquid.

It was still better than the alternative. Vedikus sighed and picked up his tools. That black cloud remained.

Her skin was inflamed, sopping wet, and exposed. Aldora arched and cringed from the pain that stabbed at her from beneath her flesh and found only a weak sense of comfort when a new pain distracted her from the other. Nausea coiled in her belly and she rolled to her side and hacked. Nothing but raw air and spittle came forth.

Then, suddenly, the pressure eased and the burning liquid pooling over her flesh sank into her wounds and flooded her insides. In a matter of moments, she went from agony to high bliss. Her tears dried up and she dropped back onto the sodden ground.

Nothing. She felt nothing but a crystalline daze that lightened her head. It *was* bliss. Even the damp ground that threatened to suck her into the earth was soothing.

Calloused, rough hands probed and pulled at her skin and she opened her eyes to watch. He didn't look at her, this beast, but concentrated on the places his hands touched. Although she knew he did something to her skin, and she could feel it being pinched and poked, it wasn't painful. There was only the sensation of pressure.

He slowly made his way up her body, leaving nothing behind but her disturbed undergarments. Steamy exhales warmed her skin as his fingers trailed hurriedly upon her. Aldora blinked slowly as he raised her elbow and brought her wrist to his nose. The rent flesh had reopened under the boiling mixture and what had stiffened over with dried blood was now exposed and fresh.

A snarling hiss left his mouth, bringing her attention back to him. "This happened on the other side." His tone was deep, threatening.

Her tongue felt heavy but she managed to speak. "When I ran...and was caught. It was a Las—Laslite patroller that discovered me. I should've run faster."

"No." He met her eyes. "If you had run faster you wouldn't be here now. I've heard of these Laslites. Are they warriors?"

Aldora tugged her hand but he held strong, ignoring her attempt, and scooped up the extra mixture from the bowl, slathering her wrist with it. "Yes," she said, upset, her world spinning. "F-fierce warriors, the best of Savadon, and they travel with the king's warrant. They would destroy you." She loathed the Laslites now as much as she distrusted him but she kept that to herself.

He dropped her wrist and picked up her other arm, showing her a massive bruise on her upper arm. "The same kind of men who would grip a soft female so hard to leave a mark such as this? Aldora, your Laslite did this intentionally," he spat as his fingers softly trailed her mottled flesh.

"And you haven't inflicted pain on me intentionally?" Aldora tried to sit up. On her third attempt, he hoisted her to a sitting position.

"I'm no Laslite man-scum," he sneered.

"You're no man at all!"

Aldora gripped the bone bowl and slowly tried to maneuver away, but was hauled roughly into a wall of muscle. She stiffened as the bowl slipped from her hand to spill over the top of her thighs. Her back was up against his naked chest and a thick arm banded hard around her belly, trapping both her arms to her sides.

A voice breezed into her ear. "What am I? Do you even know?"

She licked her lips and held still. Whatever answer she gave him, it wouldn't be the right one. That much she knew. He. Thing. It. *Horned heretical beast.* She was in a dangerous position, deep within a dangerously forbidden place, breathing in poison and losing her sense of self. Her mother's apples came to mind and how she would dig her nails deep into their skin until their juices burst to coat her fingertips, until nothing was left but sticky sweet mush.

Aldora focused on the image until she relaxed in his arms.

"I don't know what you are." She relaxed further.

His chest pressed into her, lungs expanding to move her body with each of his inhales. The rhythm and his heat accented the chilling voice in her ear. She wanted to hang onto the cold parts of him because his heat was consuming her.

Sex.

Aldora pressed her thighs together.

His hand moved up her belly and over her breast to capture her neck. A light squeeze and a tap to her chin brought his mouth to her cheek. It was wet and soft, malleable as it moved against her skin. His arms held her tight enough for her to know that even if she fought, it would be for nothing, and she had little fight left in her to begin with.

What did he give me?

He was a wall at her back and a shield of arms and legs, a being larger and stronger than she'd ever seen, with a voice that came out as a lullaby every time he spoke. His lips remained on her cheek and his hand on her neck. Aldora waited for the twisting and groping, the sudden shock of penetration as he shredded her last garment... but it never came.

Her legs shook and her core tightened with each inhalation she rode. His warmth continued to seep into her skin, followed only by more of the mixture that rearranged her world.

A muddled awareness overtook the numbing effects of it drying on her body. His hand shifted on her neck and dirty fingers swept across her lips.

"Human female flesh is soft," he said, rubbing them. "This is why you make the best breeders."

Aldora tensed but couldn't move. "Breeders?" It was a term used for certain livestock on the farm, the ones that were used to procreate. Images of them in heat flashed in her mind. She was no innocent when it came to sex, but it had always been on her terms.

"Human females who are not yet fully tainted by the mist. If taken care of and kept well, protected from the other beasts that roam this world, they will produce fresh blood and halfbreeds. They will solidify a new generation for any pack or tribe and cleanse them with new lifeforce." His hand moved back down to her neck, leaving her lips raw and pouted.

"So that's the reason?" Her words slurred. "Why Savadon is forced to sacrifice hundreds of our kind each year..." Aldora shuddered but had never stopped bracing for pain, even after the numbness.

A burst of cackling, thick laughter filled her ears and she was let go.

She barely caught herself and worked her way to the other side of the fire. The trees turned upside-down. His laughter deepened with sinister glee, taking an edge that had her searching for her discarded clothes. Aldora dragged them to her side, and with several failed attempts, eventually redressed herself.

She was no longer in pain but her skin was apple-red from the boiling liquid. She checked the bruise on her arm, finding it no more than a blemish of its former self.

"What?" she asked when he continued to cackle between toothy smiles. Aldora yanked the dagger from her boot, her hand shaking with the effort.

"It has nothing to do with your people's sadistic need to sacrifice others of your kind." He rose up on his haunches. "You appear and the rest of us in the mist take advantage. Not all beasts care about your flesh. Some just want your blood, some are just... ravenous." His eyes narrowed and she tightened her hold on her weapon. The pressure between her legs strengthened as her gaze flickered over his powerful muscles.

Aldora watched him cautiously, feeling her strength begin to return. "The mists don't encroach into our lands if we make sacrifices. That's how it's been for generations, since—"

"Forever?"

"Yes."

He leaned closer to the fire and she shifted back. He picked up the pile of plants and stuffed them into a pouch then began to string them to the buckles around his waist. "The cursed mist has no mind of its own, it cares nothing for you humans. Why else call it a curse? There's no fighting it, no bloodthirsty battle to savor."

"But it doesn't come into our lands. It stops at the labyrinth wall and stays there," she argued despite Burlox's fall coming to mind. "Humanity's kingdom remains untouched as long as humans are delivered to you. That's how it has always been, how it still is..." How she'd been raised, being told this every day living in a bordertown. Her entire world was affected by the labyrinth, each nightmare and grim thought was because of it, every morning from the first blink to evening's last. The mist was always in the back of her mind. "We battle the mist by respecting it."

So many decisions were borne from it. Everyone in Thetras, in all of Savadon, lived within the shadow of the labyrinth wall. *We have celebrations...*

Depraved, hedonistic celebrations.

Aldora rubbed her lips on the back of her hand, remembering his touch. "The mist recently overtook a town north of mine, of Thetras," she added.

"Your people think it's because of the sacrifices?" he

goaded. "There were rumors of a large influx of humans. That very reason affected your life."

"Why else would the town fall if it wasn't because it failed? What do you mean, affected my life?"

"Female, it's all because of your blood. Everything is about human blood here." He re-sheathed his axes. "Look around and see how the mist does not cling around you like it does the plants, the trees, me. It tries to and it's gaining ground second by second until it can envelop your soft flesh to conquer, but do not fret, breeder, I won't let it take away my pet."

"I'm not your—" His hand snapped out and grabbed her before the words came out, pulling her onto her feet. She pointed the dagger at the wall of his stomach, but before she could thrust it deep, one of his hands closed over hers while the other tangled in her hair. He jerked her head back and wrenched the weapon from her hand.

"Human pet," he snarled and a blast of steam hit her face. "Your kind is killing itself. The more you throw into the labyrinth, the less you have to repel the curse. One day, there will be no Savadon, no sunlight to stream through the veil, no world left for you and it's no one's fault but your own." She flinched as her hair was pulled and pain shot across her scalp. "One day, you'll all be ours and everything you've built will be gone. You'll adapt or you'll die." He released her hand and she reached back to grab the hand holding her hair, tears springing in her eyes.

"You're lying," she breathed, her lips parted. She strained on her toes in an attempt to relieve the pressure of his grip.

"Has your kingdom ever gained back any land?"

Aldora searched her mind already knowing the answer but she couldn't allow herself to believe it. She'd never heard of Savadon expanding, only shrinking, losing what was left when quotas weren't met. It didn't explain the giant, nearly impenetrable wall that connected their worlds, nor the countless ones who miraculously returned from the mists.

"No," she answered. He released her and she stumbled to her knees. She picked up the dagger between them and looked at it, not wanting to see anything else. "We've only ever lost it."

"As it will always be."

"Why tell me this? We both know I'm at your mercy, that you'll never let me go back, that I'll never even get the chance."

"Because the sooner you work with me, rather than against me, the stronger you'll become."

"The sooner you'll use me," she snapped. *He's taking me to his brothers.*

His cloven feet moved out of her line of sight and she trailed her finger across the dagger's primitive design. Aldora blinked again rapidly to clear the wayward tears on her lashes and stood, pushing the blade back into her boot, while reaching out and picking up the bone bowl. Ashes flew up into the air as he stamped out the fire.

"What," she started, lifting her eyes back to his horns, "are you?" Her gaze drifted down his body to his thick, leather loincloth and the bushy fur that covered him from his hips to his ankles.

"Vedikus."

Vedikus. His name breathed of ember and ruin, pain

and depravity. A single word said in incantation to bring the dead back to life or to enthrall the living. Vedikus. Knowing it burned the back of her throat. Aldora forced herself not to swallow. She wanted nothing of him inside of her, she realized, but she didn't have a choice.

He stepped toward her with a rope in his hand.

Chapter Eight

His fingers tightened on the leash, snapping the weaker threads in half. The female stiffened but did not flee when he tied it back around her waist. Her expression was unreadable except for the glare of cove in her irises.

Vedikus readied for a fight that never came.

She was growing used to his presence. All he had to do now was not spook her. The press of his bulge was uncomfortable against his loincloth, an unneeded distraction. It had quickened the moment he heard her voice for the first time, like a snake in preparation to strike, but had been denied with venom dripping from its mouth. He denied it now and glanced up at the sky.

The sun is at its zenith.

He pulled on the rope and she jerked forward, keeping her balance. "Your wounds are fading. How are you feeling?"

She looked up from the rope to settle her gaze back on him, mystified. "I feel nothing."

"Can you walk, or do I need to carry you?" Vedikus tried to read her but found it difficult. She stared at him without expression for another long moment. He would carry her even if it put them at a disadvantage in a surprise attack. To keep her flesh upon his was something his body craved. The more he explored her, the more she gave into him.

"I thought you admired strength."

He narrowed his eyes. "And the truth," he warned.

"I can walk."

He studied her for a second longer, before looking at the burned grass in the center of the copse and the pile of strung-out vines thrown about. The tension that barely held him together burned to be released and he clenched his hand around the rope.

High noon was the safest time of day as the worst of the beasts were night-dwellers. The ghouls and wraiths fled to the shadows even if the light was faint, and those that could not find shelter dug themselves deep into the soil. The orc drums had faded hours past. Only the horsemen would be lingering out in the light. The centaurs moved little at night unless it was deemed necessary.

If they were going to slip out from the barrier paths without notice, it would be now, before the first tendrils of evening.

Vedikus knew the female was unwell, disturbed, possibly in denial, but there was nothing more he could do for her here...

Besides keep her breathing.

He led her from the clearing without another word and back into one of the thousand endless passageways of the labyrinth. He sensed her hovering close to his back, keeping the leash slack but not near enough to touch. Not like how she had leaned on him the night before.

His tail flicked, searching for the feel of her, but caught under the flap of his leathers.

It is for the best. He was ready to mount the female and each touch of her soft skin made it worse. Just knowing she was following his shadow and trapped at his side proved difficult enough. But he would not take her to the ground, not while the mist worked its curse, not while danger loomed. If he should fill her womb with his seed and it took root and he was unable to reverse her sickness, a thrall would bear his offspring, a mindless servant.

Vedikus did not know what that would do to the young and he had no plans of ever finding out. It would mar what he and his brothers had worked so hard for: a tribe of their own.

He settled his palm over his axe and stretched the muscles in his neck. *We'll be at Prayer before dark.*

There was a hag dwelling in Prayer, a lesser Lich that would have all he needed to stop the sickness. The cove and blimwort he'd poured down her throat were good enough to stall the malignancy but not strong enough to cure it.

A hand touched his arm, bringing his thoughts to a halt.

"What's that?" she asked, looking off into the distance.

Vedikus glanced in her direction and quieted his blood, his breaths. A soft whisper drifted through the air, at first obscured by the other noises but gained quickly in strength to a piercing buzz. He reached out to grasp the back of Aldora's neck.

"Another sacrifice."

She stiffened. "From Thetras? Are we close to any other human towns?"

Vedikus hurried his steps and forced her to keep up with his lead. "No."

She stumbled after him and her grip on him returned. If the situation wasn't building in urgency he would have taken a minute to relish his victory.

"Another sacrifice," she gasped, "and so soon…"

Vedikus cursed the timing. *The longer she's connected to her people...*

The longer she would fight him.

"Wait," she pleaded. He dragged her behind him. "Wait!" It spread out like wildfire from the goblin scouts at the junction and continued on in every direction for miles to alert the swarms. By the time he had gone after Aldora the night before, most of the goblin scouts were already dead by his hands. Not anymore.

Aldora resisted his pull and struggled behind him, fighting the leash and the hand he kept clamped on her scruff. Vedikus shifted, picked her up, and threw her over his shoulder just as the others met the call. What had started out as a quiet morning was now tense with a new wave of impending battle and bloodshed.

"Let me go!" The female pulled at the armor straps across his back. "My town is sacrificing another!" Nails grazed his back and caught in his wounds. He gritted his teeth. "*Please.*"

Oh, how sweetly the human can beg.

He turned on his hoof and entered through the deep hanging vines, pulling Aldora down to thrust her back into the hedge wall. His palm covered her mouth. She arched away and he closed the distance, catching her eyes with his own in warning. Cackles and the clink of metal sounded just as she stilled. The points of his horns dug into the bark and stone above her head.

They stayed like that long after the snickers faded into the distance.

Vedikus slowly dropped his hand. She sucked in a wavering breath and clung to him. He pushed his hips forward and settled his engorged shaft against her stomach. Her nails pierced his flesh. The sounds of renewed fighting and hollers of battle rose up like wisps on every side.

"Are we close?" she whispered.

"Closer than we should be. The paths are long and winding, spreading for miles in every direction within the barrier lands. Once we make it out of this wretched place, the way opens up."

She peered over his arm to look through the thick foliage to the other wall across from them. He damned the humans of her town. Vedikus leaned over her to block her sight. A question lighted her eyes and he answered before she could voice it. "We're not going back."

The female closed her eyes and shuddered. "My town is sacrificing another. Yesterday, I was there yesterday delivering apples to the breadmaker and…" She shifted on her feet but not to move away from him. "There was no talk of a sacrifice, no criminals that had arrived from the capital."

"We're not going back."

"What if it's my fault? It's my fault." Guilt filled her

voice. *Guilt.* An emotion like hope, one that he gave no mind to. It wafted from his human in stifling waves and he drew back his hips. Regret was different, a feeling along the same vein. The distance they had lost would cost them now.

His bulge throbbed between his thighs loud enough to match his heart. *The death of me.* He released a cloud of steam. "Why? You're only at fault for yourself, not what the humans on the other side have done. Once they thrust you over that barrier, all ties are severed between you and them. You may not have wanted it, but they decided for you."

Vedikus lifted his head and glanced over his shoulder, past the vines and shadows, toward the path. *Centaur hooves approach. Not many.*

When he and the other Bathyr had split from their birth tribe, their anger had destroyed all ties to their past. It was the only way to push on.

Aldora moved and he looked back at her.

"Would you cut someone down so viciously?" she asked.

He paused. "Yes."

"Even me? Once my usefulness to you runs out?"

He would never abandon a human. He slid his hand under her chin. "The uses for humans are many. To abandon a war prize so sought after is unheard of."

"Even if I break my leg, my arms, my body?" she asked quietly.

"I would break them back into place."

She flinched. Vedikus turned away, listening to the approaching horses, guessing their distance. Whether they were on this side of the hedge wall or on the other, he was not yet sure, but the fresh smell of tainted blood permeated the air.

Telner and the two other stallions the horsebeast had been with came to mind. Vedikus could take on several centaurs at once, but more than three would be risky, and the path they were on was just wide enough to allow one to maneuver around him… if they kept him distracted.

"What if I fight you every single step of the way and every moment with me becomes a trial? What if I betray you at the first opportunity, regardless of what would happen to me? Would you leave me for dead?"

"Do you plan on betraying me?" he snarled.

Her eyes widened, large and leafy brown, searching his gaze and trying to read something in him he wasn't sure was there. His nostrils flared.

"I don't know," she answered.

His lips twitched. *The female is not entirely afraid of me.* "I will not leave you to the monsters. If you're trying to compare me to those of your kind, go ahead, but I'll never prove you right. If you're looking for a reason to run, you'll find many but you'll find more to stay."

Vedikus slammed his hand back over her mouth and twisted away, swinging one of his axes in an arch. Plants fell in strings around his arm as his blade cleaved the head straight off the scout sprinting past. Blood gushed outward as the creature crumpled to the ground, its head rolling away.

He pulled the body of the corpse into the shadows as Aldora shifted from the wall. He pulled on her leash in reminder. *Several feet is all you get.*

"It's dead," she murmured, bewildered. "I didn't even know it was there."

"A goblin scout." He didn't bother consoling her as he kneeled and picked up a crude whistle tied to the goblin's hand. "The piece that warns of a human entering the labyrinth." Vedikus lifted it to show her. When she took it from his grasp, he stood. "Blow through this hole," he pointed at the whistle's end, "in three short bursts if we ever get separated. I'll know it's you."

She turned it around and looked at the whistle mutely then tucked it into a fold on her shirt. "I'll remember."

"We're not going back," he reminded her.

"Even at the chance of another human?"

Inhuman screams arose in the distance.

"I won't risk the first."

The female glanced up at him through her messy hair. He reached up and pulled the vines and half-dead leaves from it.

"Will… they survive?" she asked.

"I don't know."

She nodded, brow furrowed, and folded hands around the rope at her hips, nodding again but didn't speak.

His ear twitched and Vedikus adjusted the grip on his axe. The sound of hooves neared. It was time to go.

"You're no longer a sacrifice," he told her, stepping away.

He pulled on her leash and moved out onto the path, checking both directions and squinting through the mist. The ground vibrated. Dead leaves fell in waves from the branches above.

They were soon running down the path in the opposite

direction. Aldora clutched at his back and he pulled her with him, jutting his head forward. His stamina was more than enough for both of them. His momentum unmatched. The passageway split into three paths.

"To the right," he yelled, yanking on the leash so that she was suddenly up against him and moving with his body. Her feet dragged for a few steps before righting herself. Vedikus heard nothing but the thunder at his back as he picked passages that would slow the centaur stampede, but the more they ran, the closer the beasts came.

"Halt or die!" one of them roared behind them. Aldora stumbled and he caught her before she fell.

"How do they know where we are? What are they?" she gasped as he hefted her up, and wrapped her legs around his waist.

"They're close enough to see the mists clear up by you. They're looking for it." He grunted as her leg rubbed over his bulge. "Centaurs," he sneered.

"What should we do?"

"Run," Vedikus barked, pulling her closer to him just as a spear shot past, narrowly missing her. Aldora clutched his side, her boots digging into his back and hip. He ducked when the whistle of several arrows flew over his head, breezing past his horns.

He dashed forward and followed the swirling mist where the spear had embedded itself into a hedge wall. Dropping his axe, he yanked it free with his open hand. The female dropped from his side and crouched behind with her dagger back in hand.

Vedikus readied the spear and waited, waited for Aldora's stolen dagger to sink into his flesh, and for the first centaur raider to appear.

"Minotaur! Vengeance will be ours," a familiar voice shrieked. "We had a deal!"

Horse hooves, sinewy chest decked in ribbons of metal and leather, followed by long, braided golden hair blowing outward appeared and Vedikus pulled his arm back. Two other studs emerged directly behind, flanking their leader, the same one he recognized from the night before. Aldora huddled behind, using him as the shield that he was as the horsemen charged toward them in full force.

"The human is ours!" the leader cried.

Vedikus sneered, knowing the commotion would draw others.

"Be ready to run," he breathed.

His muscles tense, his body balanced, his vision sharpened.

He flung the spear.

It sliced through the air and struck the leader in the center of his chest, stopping the stud like a wall. Without waiting, Vedikus snatched up his axe and grabbed Aldora. He could hear the angry roars and furious stomping behind them. He dragged the female along and cut through the paths, the distance between him and the centaurs lengthening each second.

He glanced at his female, heaving with exertion. The lax glare of the cove still apparent in her eyes. *Her slight body is not used to its magic.* He was thankful it kept her going, but for how much longer he wasn't sure.

Some creatures hunted by smell, by sounds, some by other senses he did not possess. Vedikus could smell her sweat and even to him, it smelled of humanity. Delicious humanity, ripe for the taking.

My humanity. An erotic taste bloomed on his tongue. His mouth watered, readying for more, and he released a pent-up breath of steam.

He ran with her until every last ounce of her energy was gone, until her only hope of movement was him, and as the sun began to set, he kept them moving as she sought out his strength and made it her own.

The need to keep her that way corrupted his soul.

Chapter Nine

They came to a stop at the crest of a plateau.

Below them lay the old barrier point, once when the labyrinth had been smaller. Back before he'd been born. Each year the mist covered more ground and seeped into the lands of humans, and each year the pathways and hedge mazes—the corrupted growth—sprouted from the dirt and expanded. It was something he nor any other creature could stop. The liches and giants of his world had tried.

Eventually, the mist would cover the whole of this world and no new pureblood humans would be born. Those with forethought quaked at the idea but most anticipated the final usurpation, and the endless supply of humans even if it was for such a short time. The magic and chaotic frenzy of his world looked forward to that day.

The Bathyr prepared.

Vedikus scanned the ocean of fog and jostled the female.

"Mmh-what?" Aldora struggled and he dropped her feet, keeping one arm around her. He had run them raw through the noontide, and when she could no longer hold herself upright, he'd picked her back up to keep on going. The distant sounds of bloodshed and shrieks had chased them the entire way. Dozens of goblins lay dead in their wake and he could feel their blood beginning to dry within his hooves.

"Look. What do you see?" he asked, curious. He saw nothing but the grey and the muted colors reflected from the sky. His ears twitched at her inhale of breath.

"Nothing. I see nothing but white in every direction." She looked back, her expression bleak. "Except for the growth behind us. The paths have stopped..." Aldora turned to him. "Are we going in there?"

"Yes," he answered.

She sank to the ground, wilting like dying vile leaf, and stared over the endless void without expression. Vedikus crouched beside her and pulled off her boots, revealing pale abraded feet. He swept his fingers over her ankle expecting her to jerk back and smiled when she didn't.

"Where are we?" Her voice was low. "Where are you taking me?"

He pointed off into the distance in the direction she stared. "Prayer lies within, a half day's journey from here, but it depends."

"Prayer?"

"It is a settlement outside the border paths near here, located in the middle of an endless expanse of wetlands that can be followed to the sea." He didn't like how close it was to the mountains his brothers called home.

Aldora gaped at him. "A settlement? Here? People live in this place? How is that possible?" Her sudden shock struck him and he eyed her curiously.

"Is that so hard to believe?"

"Yes…"

"Even beasts need a place to rest," Vedikus mocked. "It is not a lively place."

"Are there humans?"

A hag. Thralls. Humans? "Not anymore."

"Oh." The abrupt shock eased from her face. "Then what does it depend on?"

"On where we left the barrier paths." He propped up her other foot to slide his hands across her skin. *Fresh, tough calluses will replace her soft flesh soon.* He cupped her sole. *They will help.* She pulled her feet from his grasp and shoved them back into her boots with a wince. The numbing effect of the cove had run its course.

He rose to his feet and the female followed suit but stumbled back to her knees. She steadied herself and rose again only to fall back down. Vedikus grabbed the back of her tunic and hauled her up. "You're dead weight."

"Does it make a difference? I can keep moving."

"Perhaps, but you can't crawl down a cliff…" He led her away, helping her traverse the uneven ground. "And even if you could, you would make a perfect target for an arrow."

"I'm a perfect target for everything right now," she whispered. "I don't want to stop."

"You would travel through the twilight and onward into the dark now? Farther away from all you once knew when you begged me not long ago to go back? I'm not easily fooled," Vedikus warned. He had expected more of a fight once the dust had settled, once he had shown her the world beyond. It was a terrorizing view, being at the brink of a shrouded world without being able to see into it, not knowing what lay within. Only knowing more horrors awaited.

It was home to him. He was bred on top of old bones and furs, the mist licking at his newborn body.

All he knew of Savadon and his female's world was what he had been told by his mother and the occasional wanderer. That life in the light was easy, that it had a softness to it and that humans brought that softness into the labyrinth where it didn't belong. He also knew that softness was begotten by corruption and delusion. *Oh, the deviousness of humans.*

He could be devious too.

Vedikus gazed back over the colorless mist, picturing the bog that was soon to be in their future. If he peered hard enough he could almost imagine the toothy, jagged mountains on the other side and even harder still, the green lights that would indicate the trails leading into and out of Prayer.

"If I stop," she rasped, "my thoughts will become the thing I focus on and I don't think I can bear them. I never got to say goodbye to my…"

"To who?" Vedikus urged. Was there a male in her life? He had not thought about it before and gripped Aldora tighter. *Another male.* The need to feel hot blood bubble up between his hands quickly overcame him. The ground sloped and he quickened his steps.

"My family." Her voice was laced with sadness.

He heard her say the words but the black cloud filled his skull. It was a dark thing that had a mind of its own. One he easily succumbed to and one he usually only felt in the throes of battle, at the zenith of a berserker rage. The thought of something taking away his prize and claiming it for themselves infuriated him. Not because he felt something for the human female, that anything she had to offer wouldn't someday be his, but that his power over her might be affected.

"You have no family now, only me," he growled.

"I'm only a means to an end with you. One I'll accept because you haven't hurt me, but that will never change the fact that I have a family out there, one that I'll miss for the rest of my life... however long it is."

Vedikus pulled Aldora after him and off the rocky slope and into a circle of boulders and ruins deteriorating on the cliff's edge. "And yet you don't want to stop long enough to think about them. Is missing them so painful?" He never missed his brothers, only their usefulness on occasion.

"Yes," she breathed at his side.

He gritted his teeth and moved them deeper into the old ruins.

Crumbling stones covered in moss quickly surrounded them as he made his way through, listening for any beasts or monsters that may have made camp. There were old tools and broken wares piled up throughout from passing bands, and the deeper he moved into the ruins, the more the old stone walls were covered in symbols and spellcasts. Whether they were put there with paint or dried blood he wasn't sure and didn't stop to investigate. There would be leftover magic lingering and if it were dark magic, he did not want to spend the effort to clear it out. Not while he had a female to take care of.

They stopped short of where the shadows began. "From here and until daybreak you'll think of nothing but me." Vedikus picked up the cord that he'd let fall and tugged her close. "Do you understand, female?" Her body shuddered in response.

"Aldora," he warned, grasping her hair and forcing her to face him.

Tears glistened her eyes. Vedikus scrutinized them, appreciating the amber sparkle they made. A feature he wanted his future bull-sons to have.

"I'd rather be sad and thinking of them than give any more of myself to you!"

"You've given nothing of yourself to me." He squeezed her flesh.

She wrested from his hold and he let her go. "I've given you my life, my life and my trust, and how could I? You're not even human."

"Your life was never yours to give, only to take, and I have taken it. It is mine, female." He turned back to the passageway that led deeper into the ruins, deeper into the ledge, letting his rage cool. "You will give your thoughts to me tonight and I'll ask nothing more from you. Wait here." He left her to return outside, ripping armfuls of vines and blisterwood from the gnarled overhanging trees before hefting a boulder to block the entrance. When he returned, he found her sitting against a broken wall, rubbing her calves.

She stood, using the wall for support as he approached.

"Follow me," he ordered, bringing the blisterwood to his lips and lighting it on fire.

Darkness consumed them quickly and the air grew colder with each step. His hooves clacked against the stone, splitting them as he moved through. Aldora followed behind him obediently and he wondered if she had really given him her trust.

The ruins veered off into rooms that were covered in webs and nests, some of which he burned down as they passed. The smoke drove the smaller critters away. Aldora clutched his back at one point as they continued through.

It wasn't until the trickle of water could be heard that he stopped. Vedikus moved to the source and scouted the small space he had chosen. The room was deep within the ruins, in the ground, which had its advantages and disadvantages, but there was no such thing as true safety at night in the mists. Death prowled the land after dusk in a myriad of forms.

He placed the blisterwood in the center of the space and well away from the water flowing down the wall. He slipped his hand in the water where it pooled at the bottom before it flowed away into the stones below.

"Is it fresh?"

"As fresh as it could be but cold enough to freeze your skin." He lifted his numb hand away and checked out the rest of the room. It was more of a cave than it was a space created by humans. All the ruins in his land had been created by humans long ago, landmarks of the past. Vedikus looked for ghosts.

"Do you still have your bone bowl?" she asked.

He grunted and loosened his pouches, setting them by

the fire, and handed her the bowl when it was free. Without pause, she had cleansed it and made use of it to drink. He watched Aldora fill it again and again, drinking deep of the water, her throat contracting with each swallow. The fire casting a soft glow on her skin. His ever-persistent shaft twitched, and he wiped his hands across his leathers.

We're safe this nightfall. Some of the tension drained from his muscles and he built up the fire.

Even the barghests cannot be heard here. He unsheathed his axes and set them aside. His ears twitched when the water splashed and soothing, breathy noises teased them.

Vedikus shut his eyes and clenched his fists. "Aldora." Those sounds stopped. He felt her gaze. "Take off your clothes."

She stared, transfixed, at her captor's haloed outline, the shadows created by the dim light accentuating his horns. They seemed to lengthen with each flicker of the flames, elongating and sharpening. *Soon they'll pierce the ceiling like they do the dark. The sky.* Aldora fingered the bowl in her hand, frightened and yet… relieved.

She looked around at the dark corners as she straightened, feeling the water trail down her arms, clearing her skin of sweat and grime.

"Fill the bowl with water and bring it here," he commanded. Each request he made of her caused her to hesitate but she knew, after a day, that each would be answered. Aldora filled the bowl and moved to his side.

She placed it before him and stepped back out of his line of sight, bringing her now-empty hands up to play with the hem of her clothes.

"You said you would ask for nothing but my thoughts tonight," she said.

He emptied one of the pouches of herbs and dunked it into the bowl. "I don't want your clothes, I want you to take them off." His voice was gruff, but he did not look her way.

"And after that?" she asked, hating that her belly coiled sharp enough to make her core ache. She was aware of his shaft, thick and pointed just beneath his loin-cloth. Her gaze had caught sight of it throughout the day. It had not diminished even when he killed, cleaving creatures' limbs off, and as she swallowed, feeling a hungering hollowness, a wrongness at what was happening, she was aware that sex *would* happen. She'd felt helpless all day knowing it was coming, that this horned beast was taking her somewhere far from everything she knew to make her his breeder.

That she was sick and he had the means to cure her.

That she had not been able to smell anything since the night before.

That he had not hurt her once, despite her giving him reasons to do so, when everything about him was violent and relentless. In his presence, she was lucky to be alive.

"After that, I'll feed you," he said, startling her. *Feed me?* Food had barely entered her mind, not with everything else vying for the space; fighting with all those little haunting thoughts that wanted her attention. Her predicament. Her life. The cruelty of the Laslites and the Master of Thetras severing her from everything she'd known. Aldora fisted her hands into her tunic. *The second sacrifice.*

There will be many more to come. The thought saddened her. She only hoped those who came after her were deserving of their fate, and that other innocents like herself would find a captor like—

Aldora refused to finish the thought, her gaze on Vedikus's ever-sharpening horns. They danced in the shadows, rising up and falling back down to their normal shape. They were paler than the rest of his body and reflected light and darkness equally back to her.

"Feed me?" she asked lamely, taken aback, still unsure.

"You do need food like any living being?" he teased.

"I do." She swallowed and kneeled at his side. "I wasn't expecting it."

"Why?"

"You just asked me to take off my clothes."

"And yet...you still haven't."

A blush warmed her cheeks and she turned away. She didn't want him to see it.

Her body ached, wrung out from the constant, stressful fleeing for her life. It seemed like an eternity had passed since she had last been in Thetras, had last spoken to another human, and those final memories of her kind only filled her with anger. She gritted her teeth. *Betrayal.*

Aldora rubbed her arm where the Laslite hurt her, where his mark still remained. Even when she'd gone numb, she could still feel the pounding bruise below her clothes, could still feel the way the patrollee had groped and threatened her, how it hadn't stopped until they were at the top of the sacrificial stairs on the outskirts of town.

There had been no remorse from the man, and the press of his fingers at the center of her back made her want to tear off her skin.

She felt them now. A sudden, single violent shiver wracked her frame.

I don't want to be in my head! It didn't make the memory of his touch go away.

A large calloused hand took her own. "Female... Are you hiding something from me?"

She stared down at Vedikus's fingers curling around her palm, overly warm, and slightly damp from the bowl. Another tremor coursed through her but this one wasn't from disgust. She turned her hand in his and trailed her thumb over his cracked knuckles, waiting for her revulsion, but it never came. He had gone still beneath her fingertips and another tendril of relief flowed through her.

Aldora grasped his wrist, unable to wrap her fingers fully around it, and squeezed. A thick tendon protruded from his skin and rose up his bare underarm. She spread her fingers upon his other hand and moved them from his blunt nails and over his rough pads, to the curve of his thumb and the tough skin where he held his weapons, further still to meet her other hand holding his wrist.

The more she touched him, the more she relaxed. Heat from the fire filled the space between them and warmed the stones she sat upon. Aldora pressed her palm against his and the tops of his fingers curled down over her outstretched ones.

"I'm not hiding anything," she whispered.

"Then remove your clothes."

The spell was broken. Aldora snatched her hand back

and rubbed the feel of him off her. His hand hovered in the air between them for another moment before dropping to the forgotten bowl.

"I don't want to," she said. Even with the heat from the fire now keeping her warm, she didn't want to, not even knowing she had a chance to wash the blood and mud from her body and clothes made her want to take them off.

They were her last—maybe her only—physical barrier against him. The dagger that lay hard against her ankle wasn't enough to make her feel completely safe. She rubbed her palms into her clothes again but couldn't get the feel of him off of her. That singular roughness remained.

Vedikus removed a root from a bag and twirled it in the flames. "You don't have a choice."

Her nostrils flared and she slid her hand toward her boot. He pulled the singed herb from the flame and crushed it into the water. The powder vanished within the mixture.

"I have a choice." She slipped the weapon out, raising it to strike, staring at his exposed back and shoulder. He made no move as she poised the crude tip against his skin, her arms shaking. He swirled the bowl, mixing the contents. Her palms dampened.

And she lowered the dagger. "I can't," Aldora breathed.

He looked at her then, and she braced for violence, but only received the damning intensity of his gaze. There was little space between them, no more than a foot, and she drew back as the darkness in them grew. Their pits swirled and burst with each quick rise of the fire, deepening them with each passing second. Her lips parted to be wetted. Her tongue was not up for the job.

"Even if you had stabbed me…" he trailed off, his voice as deep as his eyes.

Vedikus knocked the dagger aside and placed the bowl beside her, but she her attention was on his wet fingers grasping her legs and pulling them out from under her.

"You would not have won," he finished.

"I wasn't trying to win." His large hands slowly moved down her thighs, across her knees, and along her shins, trailing heat with them over her clothes. "I wanted to see if I could do it."

"You couldn't." He pulled off her boots.

A part of her wanted to reach out and touch him again, to see if he would let her explore more but stopped herself. *I just tried to stab him, maim him, maybe even kill him. I've given him trust.* To her chagrin, there was trust, and she couldn't believe in it. *Keeping me alive has nothing to do with trust.* And yet, she trusted him in that.

"I don't know my way out of here without you," she argued. Vedikus stuffed his hands into her boots and felt around before lifting them to his nose. "Why are you doing that?" Her brow furrowed.

He placed them next to her dagger. "I can discern a lot by smell. Your sweat is laced with many things, your blood more, and your boots reek of both. You are keeping something from me."

Aldora didn't want to answer him. She sniffed the air instead, already knowing she couldn't smell a thing. The only smell that lingered was his. "And the mist sickness?"

"Is worsening, female, far quicker than it should. What

are you keeping from me? I will not ask again and I grow tired of prying." He seized her feet and moved them into his lap.

She placed her palms on the floor and scraped her nails over them, unsure of what to tell him. He wanted something from her but all she had were her thoughts and feelings, and they were *her* secrets to keep.

"I don't like that I trust you, even a little," she said at last. A warm, moist cloth, moved across her soles, followed by his hands. She curled her toes and swallowed. "I see my nightmares every time I look at you. I see everything that has scared me all the years I've been alive. I see every reason why I made all the choices I had growing up." Hypathia sitting stiffly on Nithers leg, his hand pulling down the girl's tunic rose in her head. How Aldora was forced to do the same with other men in town. "Humans are raised to fear everything that has to do with the labyrinth."

He grunted and kneaded the aches in her arches.

Aldora remained frozen. "I made a lot of hard choices growing up because of it, every girl does. And it made no difference."

"Because it didn't save you," he agreed.

"No. They didn't save me."

"I saved you."

Her breaths stilled. "If it weren't for you I wouldn't be here."

A twisted smile curved his lips before vanishing. "No, you wouldn't." His hands moved up her legs, pushing her pants up with them. The water was cold on her skin. Her legs fell open slightly as his shadow loomed over her, and the outline of his horns pierced the ceiling once again.

"Will you hurt me?" she asked cautiously, her chest tight.

"Will you try and stab me again?"

She pondered briefly. "I don't know."

He slid his hands higher, bringing the cloth with them until the bunched up material of her pants stopped him. An empty, hollow ache built between her legs, a reaction she couldn't stop even though she hated it. *It helps. It helps the betrayal.*

His touch did not make her feel the same way the Laslite's touch had. There was no disgust, only anticipation. What pressed against his leathers at the crux of his legs, Aldora could only imagine, but she knew instinctively that it was hers to tame. *Would his prick look like a man's?* If not in size, at least in shape? Vedikus wasn't a human, not fully.

That he wasn't a man didn't bother her at all. She had never liked men before the Laslite, and she liked them even less now. They were only of use to the frightened women and girls of her town because of their fear of what lay beyond, just out of sight. Her dealings with them had always been quick, brief, and exploitative. Mutual. But only in the sense that women needed them to destroy that piece of themselves and most men took full advantage of that.

He drew his hands off her.

Her breath returned, her stillness eased, and he handed her back the dagger. Aldora took it slowly, narrowing her eyes.

"If you don't know, try again."

What? She looked at the weapon, then back to him. The dagger was heavier now. The weight unbalanced. His shadow enveloped her, his eyes lost in the dark. Aldora raised herself up, shifting the weapon in her hand. Her heels pressed into the stone, and she curled her toes.

She poised the dagger at his throat, and moved it until the tip of the blade was at his eye. He didn't look at it—but at her, unafraid despite the blade an inch from his face. Her hand began to shake.

I...can't...

Aldora slowly lowered the dagger, discovering something she didn't like.

I can't.

"You trust me too," she marveled softly.

Vedikus laughed abruptly and rose to stand, leaving her kneeling on the stone before him. Her eyes widened. He grasped her hair in his fist. "Oh, I'll hurt you, little human, but you'll be better for it in the end. Wash up." His voice lowered with warning. "Do what needs to be done. Tomorrow we head for Prayer and its toils will be worse still. I'll be back when you're done." Vedikus released her and stormed away.

He disappeared into the shadows without another word.

Aldora listened to his steps until they were gone too, and for the first time since being sacrificed, she didn't want to be alone. Didn't want her captor to leave.

Her captor...

My savior. The weight of her thoughts threatened to

crush her. She clasped the hem of her shirt. *I couldn't kill him and he trusts me.*

The revelation stayed with her as she peeled out of her dirty tunic, pants, and boots, leaving her undergarments on for safety. She washed them in the water, wringing out the dirt and scrubbing off the dried sweat and blood. Aldora draped them on a protruding stone to dry by the fire.

And with deft movements and her senses heightened— listening for his return—she took the bowl and bathed in the frigid spring. Her flimsy cloths plastered her skin. She quickly scrubbed her flesh raw in an effort to rub out her traitorous desires.

He saved me. She frowned.

She couldn't deny it and glanced at the doorway. Aldora scrubbed harder.

Her undergarments came last, her pulse strumming, as she stripped off the final barrier. She prepared for Vedikus to spring from the darkness and pin her to the ground. To exert his control and fill her head with wicked imaginings.

But as the air breezed over her drying skin, and while she cleaned her final article of clothing, his attack never came. The ache inside her would remain a secret.

Aldora redressed in her wet under layer, bearing the cold water. Time passed on well after she was done, until she lay on her side by the fire, her wet garments clinging to her skin.

Her eyes found the doorway again.

He'll come back.

She waited for his return but slumber found her first.

Aldora woke up to the darkness and cold, to the shuffling of her captor in the shadows where she could no longer see. His presence moved over and around her, slinking in like the mists she had known her whole life. *I can't see him.* And yet she knew he was right there.

The power that emanated from him brushed her skin, lifting the hairs on the back of her neck. The dirt crunched next to her ear.

"Tell me your secret." His voice slithered into her ear, inhuman. Her sex clenched.

This is a nightmare. She was certain her small bedroom would appear with its wooden walls and crates of apples in the corner.

"No."

"I will pry them out of you." His voice was at her throat now. "Will tear them out from the outside in." His breath warmed her still-damp clothes. "And replace them with my own." The heat of his mouth moved down her belly. She parted her thighs as she felt him move over her. He took hold of her legs and pulled off her wet garments before spreading limbs wide. The air touched parts of her that it shouldn't.

She was helpless and sensed that he enjoyed that, that she had nothing to worry about except for him.

There were no other monsters trying to kill her here, deep within the ground. The walls on every side were solid and impenetrable, even to those sounds she heard roaring above. It was almost like a bubble, one only a single beast was allowed entry to. Her body shook over the stone.

Thick, blunt fingers played across her sex, shocking her with the warmth of his touch.

This isn't a nightmare. Her eyes widened as she clawed at his hands, pulling them away, closing her legs as far as they could go. Aldora pressed them into his sides, arching her back in an attempt to escape him. His laugh filled her ears and echoed back. He reared up over her as she moved to get away.

Vedikus caught her up in his arms and grazed his fingers down her arm. They left a slick trail in their wake. She squirmed and fought his power, pushing off and away from his large body, her heart and ears pounding. But the more she struggled, the more he slid his hands over her and explored her body. Within moments he had her pinned over his lap, his hand palming her backside. He squeezed her flesh and she dug her nails into his leg.

"Vedikus!" she gasped as he spread her cheeks apart.

His hands stilled. "So that is how I get you to say my name." His laughter was replaced with a growl.

Aldora bit her tongue, anxious as she waited for his next move. He let out a sigh she felt throughout her whole body and ran his hand not down, but up along her spine to thread his fingers into her long hair. He fisted it and drew her face up to his.

She licked her lips as he positioned her to straddle him. She was still unable to see him, no matter how hard she tried. Her fingers came up to clutch his arms.

"Say it again," he demanded.

"Vedikus." His name slithered through her prone figure to penetrate the hollow ache between her thighs, filling her, stretching her out past the point of comfort. His arm wrapped around her lower back and pressed her against his lap. Her exposed sex rubbed over his loincloth. Aldora shuddered as she was settled over his large bulge. *He's not inside me yet.* The thought was weak in her head.

"It sounds painful on your lips." He released her hair.

"Because it is," she said, adjusting herself, but no matter how she sat on him, his shaft pushed into her. "Vedikus," she spat.

His sinister laughter filled the space once again, jostling her upon him. A pressure built in her core, each sensation pulling taut where their bodies threatened to join. Her nerves frayed beyond repair.

"I will not breed a sick female," he said when he was done cackling. "But I would fuck one."

Aldora didn't believe him but sagged in his arms at the mention of her illness. *It's gotten worse. How?* Nothing else had changed. "You came upon me in the dark."

Another growl. "I'll always come upon you then."

His bulge jerked and an unwanted jolt of pleasure surged through her.

"Always."

Chapter Ten

Aldora ate while he packed up. The sweet scent of charred meat filled the room until it became cloying and thick. The stone walls were coated with the residue of it. Her chewing filled his ears and the space tightened around him.

Vedikus palmed the handle of his axe with one hand and squeezed the grime out of the washcloth; brown and murky water gushed between his fingers. The female studied him as he washed his body. A strange tension had formed the night before, and even when he broke contact and relit the fire, it had only grown.

The pressure between his legs built and it was becoming harder to ignore. Now that he had spread her thighs and discovered the soft flesh hidden within, ignoring it was the last thing he wanted to do.

She is unlike a female minotaur, even a half-breed. He swiped the cloth down his chest and flicked the water away before it soaked into his leathers. The females that belonged to his old tribe had never fought off the need for sex. It was a natural bodily act, a ritual for his brethren. There were always willing females to curb the needs of the bulls, and mountings were revered among his kind. If there was sex, there was a possibility of creating a mating link, which meant offspring.

But there had been no links since his childhood, and he and his brothers had little to no recourse when they came of age. As the years continued and no sons and daughters were birthed, the tension in the tribe had increased.

Vedikus listened to the trickle of the spring and for any other sign that meant enemies had found them. His ears twitched, hearing only *her*.

Aldora sat near the fire, watching him through the strands of her long hair. He squeezed the cloth in his fist, wishing it was her silken hair in his grip.

"Come here." He held his hand out toward her. She stiffened and frowned but closed the distance, ignoring his hand. "Wash my back."

Her body heat, slight as it was, rushed over his skin like a wave. Vedikus hummed somewhere in his chest, feeling their connection strengthening.

Mount me. His gaze blurred slightly as she moved around him, peeling the cloth out of his hand. When she touched it to his shoulder, he lowered his head in pleasure. The act sent a rush of blood through his horns.

Streams of frigid water dribbled down the curves of his back. His focus was lost to everything else but the way it felt. Aldora washed it then patted the old water away, softening her touch around his wounds.

Her breath hitched. "Some of these…" her fingertip

caressed the skin above one of the gashes, "some of these are still open."

"They will heal." *Keep your hands upon me.*

"How can you be so sure? Does your kind heal differently than mine?" Another cold rush of water fell across his back.

"We're harder to take down and even harder to kill," he mumbled, one hand still on his weapon. "Minotaurs are more resilient than most beasts in the mist. My skin is tough and layered with extra muscle and sinew to give a natural barrier, and my bones are nearly unbreakable. Some of the most prized weapons and tools of the goblin and centaur tribes are made from the bones of my kin."

"Doesn't that bother you? Monsters are carrying around the bodies of your ancestors."

"The mist has no patience for sentimentality."

"You haven't answered my question. I know you're hard to kill...but to heal? Wounds like these would fell a human, but they would also scab over by now, or at least stop you enough so that you're forced to heal. Do you feel pain?"

"Pain," he snorted, "I feel it now." Her hands stilled upon him. "We heal but everything must run its course."

He barely stopped himself from grabbing her when she stepped away from him, heading for the fire. She tugged open several of his pouches.

"Where's that herb that you used on me? The one that cleared out my cuts and numbed the pain." Aldora looked at her wrists then returned to her search. "I'll tend to your back."

Vedikus dunked both his hands into the water. "My

wounds do not bother me." They helped him focus on something other than Aldora and the ache of his bulge. His shaft pulsed. *I need the pain.* "If you are done eating, we should finish our descent while the light persists."

"No!" She grabbed his arm and stopped him from rising. "Let me do this. Show me how to do this." Aldora caught his eyes, her hair falling from her face to clear his view of her. Her brown eyes held his, still as clear as the first time he saw them and he saw himself in them. He stilled as he looked at himself through her, until she leaned away and snatched her hand back.

He had not seen his image in many years. *I do not look the way I remembered.* Vedikus settled back onto the stone floor. "The herb you're seeking is gray and spiraled, like lichen."

She laid the materials from his bags onto the floor next to him. One by one he named them. "Wetwort eases your muscles, mossrock stops infection and is used for cleaning, the blimbery clears your head, and that," he pointed to the red leaves, "is cove and numbs the body. Grab the bowl."

Aldora retrieved it to set among the plants. "I don't recognize any of these. None of this grows in Thetras."

"Everything is warped by the mist."

"Even me."

Vedikus grabbed her hand, and pressed his thumb to her wrist, feeling her pulse. "Not yet, not after today's light." She frowned again but nodded. He did not like seeing her hopeless like this. *If she is to be helpless, it will be because of me.* "Prayer has what we need." He filled the bowl with water and handed it back to her. "Heat this up."

120

Aldora placed the bowl near the fire. "What is Prayer? Does something grow there that you're missing?"

"Something is there that we're missing, but it is not grown. Prayer is a dark spot in the labyrinth where a hag resides. A thrall who had given birth to a human within the mist, which is where most thralls come from—"

"There are humans born here?"

"Yes. They are nothing but blights and incubators with mist taint in their blood from the moment of being conceived—"

"But there are humans, humans who have known nothing else?" Excitement edged her voice.

"Thralls," he corrected. "They are not humans, not like how you know your kind. You will not find what you're wanting to find with them." There was nothing but *him* now. His fingers twitched.

"I don't understand, they are human though? And they live here?"

"Yes. Most are born here, but there are some that ended up here, like you. You will not like the sight of them."

"Because they are sick? I will like the sight of my own kind," she snapped. "I'm glad we don't all end up dead."

Vedikus narrowed his eyes. "There are worse fates."

They glared at each other and he dared her to say it, to say her fate was worse. A blush appeared on her cheeks, darkening her sun-kissed skin alluringly to a color that was not in his world. He wanted to run his tongue across it and take it into himself.

She swallowed and broke eye contact. "If I become one—"

"You won't."

"But if it were to happen...what would happen exactly?" She fingered the plants.

"You'll lose your senses, and you'll no longer feel the same as you do now. Everything becomes buried under a thick shroud. Your body is taken over by the curse and the curse doesn't die. You'll survive in pallor, in a nothingness, until your shell is destroyed. You'd be of use to no one but those who seek to harm you."

Aldora nodded. Vedikus bowed his head and tipped the points of his horns back down in submission.

She does not know what I do. He did it because she did not know. His prick ached.

"Bring back the bowl," he growled. The water bubbled, just breaking the edge of a simmer when she lowered it by the herbs between them.

"What now?"

"Take the mossrock and the cove and add it to the water." He pulled out several dried flowers, no bigger than his finger. "Crumble these up to bind the materials and mix it. The water will turn green when it's done."

"Is that all?"

His lips curled. "Unless you'd like to add some of your blood to strengthen it. Human blood is wanted for a reason. Your essence is anathema to the mist, however, nothing can remain pure in this place, as everything that is enveloped in it changes. Soon the mist will bind you to itself. Our focus now is to make sure that it does so with your mind and spirit intact." Aldora stopped swirling the bowl for a moment at his words, and to his shock, pulled the dagger from her boot. She winced as she slid the blade over her palm. The blood dripped into the mixture and made it a murky brown.

"Is that enough?"

Vedikus stared at the mixture, hungering. "Yes," he rasped. "More than enough."

Aldora cleaned his wounds then ran her hands across his back, bringing the sodden cloth with them. Her touch was gentle and the water was cool against his heated skin. It wasn't marked with pain or torment which he so readily felt, but of something else, something he hadn't known in many years. It calmed him. The water slithered off him to pool on the stone floor around his hooves.

He could feel her pure blood seeping into his cuts, destroying the rot and empowering his body.

I should not let myself get distracted. His chin hit his chest. *Just because we are safe now, does not mean we will remain safe.* His hands loosened at his sides. *Don't let them...win.*

"They're healing," she gasped. He barely heard her through the fog. She caressed her fingers over his spine. "Faster than my own wounds."

"Your blood."

"That can't be it. Blood is blood. If human blood was truly magic, Savadon wouldn't spend it so freely."

"Woman, if only you knew."

Vedikus turned on her as he rose to his feet. He gazed down at her with eyes darker and fuller than before, with no white in them at all. The sudden change left her uncertain. The hair on her neck rose.

He won't hurt me. She'd come upon that realization after he touched her. That they were both changing the longer they were together. Aldora pressed her hands to the floor, still gripping the cloth. It had numbed her fingers and softened her pads. Years of hard work, skin calloused from tending her mother's farm, had been reversed in minutes.

A plume of steam rushed from his nostrils. It rose up in white tendrils over his eyes and around his horns, lapping at the razor-sharp bone. He made no move toward her, and her eyes slipped down briefly to where his shaft poked at his loincloth. She could still feel it press against her sex, feel it wanting entry into her, could feel the pressure radiating off him in waves. It made it hard to breathe, hard to think clearly.

It was a threat that lingered in the space between them. Her thighs clenched. There wasn't an hour now that she didn't imagine the burn of his body penetrating hers.

"Is my blood that powerful?" She swallowed around her words.

He released another bout of steam to play at his horns. Her hands ached to touch them, to wipe the condensation building along their curves. *Will our children have horns?* The thought stopped her. Sweat formed on her brow.

"Yes." His voice came out hoarse. The fire crackled.

Aldora rose slowly to her feet, wincing from the lingering stiffness in her frame, and faced Vedikus head on. "Do you want more?" she asked, trying to figure the monster out.

The darkness in his eyes cleared abruptly, and his breaths cleared of heat. The tension wafting off him vanished as if it had never been there to begin with. "No."

She watched mutely as he downed the water in the bowl and licked the remaining drops off the edges. Aldora glanced at her sliced palm but blood no longer seeped from it. She wrapped the wet cloth around her wound.

In minutes they had broken camp. The herbs made their way back into pouches that now hung on his hips, his weapons were sheathed, and the fire was stomped out. Small, dusty slivers of light fell from cracks farther down the corridor leading away from their camp, and Vedikus moved toward them.

"Are you going to leash me again?" Aldora asked, catching up to him.

"Is it necessary?"

"No."

"Then I will not."

The light brightened and the air warmed as they walked further from their space. When the sting of her eyes adjusting began, Aldora glanced back at the shadows she was no longer within. The mist pooled around the corners of her vision but only small tendrils quested towards her. The bulk of the mist remained just out of reach. Waiting. Biding.

She brought a finger to her lips and dabbed at it with her tongue, already knowing what she would taste.

"Aldora."

She turned back to Vedikus, snapping out of her fugue. He stood central beneath a stone archway, a black figure that stopped the light from casting through from behind. Already, she could hear the near and distant sounds of the creatures out of her view. Wiping her hands on her pants, she moved toward him, anxious for the silence once again.

He remained motionless, watching her as she reached for his hip and tugged the rope from where it was hooked, letting the coarse threads run across her palms. The mist licked at the stone wreckage and overgrown moss at their sides, shielding them even while out in the open, hiding them from the world's view.

For a moment, it made her feel safe, protected.

The curse hides me, hides us. The murk of this place gave her a freedom she had never known. Aldora hooped the rope around his waist and tied it together, leaving the excess out for her to hold. He remained still as she tugged and tried her knot.

"I don't want us to get separated," she said, refusing to meet his eyes. "If something should happen." The thought left her mouth dry. Part of her wanted to backtrack into the ruins and find their camp again, to sit by the fire and hide.

I'm always hiding. Vedikus turned around and walked out into the open without a word. *I was good at hiding.* The rope grew taut in her grip and she followed it—him—away from the shadows.

Before him.

The view that met her was different from the night before.

Her eyes remained on his scarred back as they made their descent.

Chapter Eleven

Aldora licked her lips, lifting the back of her hand to swipe her tongue across her skin. She stayed a step behind Vedikus and well within his shadow as the path narrowed halfway down the cliff. His shoulder scrapped across the rocky ledge, dislodging dirt, moss, and shriveled, long-dead overgrowth with each step.

She refused to look out over the foggy ocean as they made their way deeper within the gorge and squeezed the rope tighter in her fist. It became her lifeline.

Don't let go. Even though the mist had cleared around her, she was still afraid it would envelop *him* whenever the rope tightened. She accepted it for what it was: survival. Nothing else mattered.

She turned her wrist and tasted her palm.

Vedikus grunted and stopped as part of the ledge crumbled and broke away under his hooves. Aldora slapped her hand against the wall and clutched the roots hanging from it. They wiggled against her palm and into her cut. She jerked her hand back. The rocks fell quickly out of sight and into the white void below. Her stomach roiled.

The rope tugged and they continued on.

"When will it end?" she asked after a while. Her voice seemed louder than usual.

"When it does."

"Haven't you been here before? You seem to know exactly where we're going." Her eyes darted from his shoulders to the path at her feet. It had begun to change from that of stone back to one of dirt.

"There are many paths through the labyrinth, more so than any being can memorize, but for me... I know these lands. The smell, the sounds, the way the light falls through the mists, and the direction is always ours for the taking. The shape of the land can't easily change."

"So you do know where we're going?"

"Yes."

She didn't have it in her to pry, not when she believed him. But it did not stop her from checking her surroundings constantly, trying to get a lay of the land. It all appeared the same; a cloudy haze swirled over everything in her periphery at all times. Whether it be a row of dying trees, a stone monolith, or a hedge wall, after awhile, it was all the same. She was directionless here.

Aldora peered over the edge once more, her stomach jumping with unease. *Endless brume.* She reached forward and rested her hand on Vedikus's back to steady herself. His body tensed under her fingers before they continued on.

Eventually, after what seemed like an eternity, her soles

hit flat ground and the ledge path widened. Her boots sank into moist soil, and the ground became thick with long stalks of grass the farther they moved away from the stone cliff. Vedikus pulled her toward the grass and tore several of the flowery bulbs growing atop them off.

"What are those for?" she asked.

"These plants are dyes. Willow growth. They stain red." He pocketed the flower tops and moved on, deeper into the grasses.

"How is that good for anything here?" She stepped gingerly as the weeds thickened, each rustle sending flies and other critters scurrying away.

"Here? Nothing, but for blood magic, it's quite useful. Mist-spawned willow growth can be ground to a paste and mixed with human blood without reducing the blood's efficacy. This has been used by warlocks for decades to extend the lifespan of human slaves, as less blood can be used for each ritual. The mixture is delicate and must be protected from the sun, otherwise, the blood-paste will harden inside the ritual warding and the spell will backfire, often catastrophically. It is highly valued."

She licked her lips. "Magic is forbidden," she said. "In Savadon, only witches use it, and to be caught... Most do not live long enough to be sacrificed."

Vedikus snorted. "Not every one of your criminals become a sacrifice?'

Aldora shook her head. "No...some are too dangerous to keep around long enough for that."

I'd been accused of witchery. And she had done nothing otherworldly or out of the ordinary except hearing a voice in the darkness. She spent her entire life walking the border path, and the sounds that came from beyond had always been garbled and animalistic, incomprehensible, and unnerving.

Her eyes drifted back to her captor, his tall outline caressed lovingly by the fog. She watched the flexing of his muscles, the horns atop his head. His tail flicked back and forth, causing eddying swirls of mist to spin lazily around his thighs.

She wanted to touch it but didn't dare.

His hand rested on the large axe hanging off to one side as he peered forward. Aldora followed his gaze and saw nothing but the grass getting higher before it vanished. There was nothing else around them. No landmarks, no walls, nothing but the same open grass field in every direction.

"My mother was a witch."

His words startled her. *He's here. If there's nothing else to follow… he's still here.* "Your mother?" she asked, curious.

"She was a human, like you, sacrificed by her people for a crime she very much committed."

Aldora looked from where his hooves were hidden then up to his horns. "Your mother was…a human?"

Our offspring will be…

"Yes. My bull father was determined to become the next chief of his tribe and sought to win through conquest and prowess. He, with several of his brothers, traversed to the wall to capture human breeders and bring them back. He returned with my mother—filled with his seed and mated—pregnant with my elder brother Thyrius, and won his claim to lead."

Aldora placed her free hand on her stomach. She shuddered with the imagery.

"How does that work?"

Vedikus turned to look at her, wearing an expression she couldn't read. "How does what work?"

Her mouth was suddenly dry. "A human and... and someone like you?"

"A minotaur."

"You've said this word before. Is that what you are?"

"I am part bull and part human, female." He smirked, dryly. "Would you care to find out?"

Aldora stared at his marred, pale flesh, and considered everything that was different between them. The ache from earlier returned between her legs. *I've never heard of minotaurs.* Although she remembered the word being yelled on the first night. *Part bull, part human.* An image of the beasts on her farm arose, making her blush.

His smile grew as her eyes dropped from his horns to settle on his loincloth, where his stiff shaft was outlined by his coverings. The tall grass swayed and tugged at her pants.

"Your father was a bull?" It was hard to get the words out.

His eyes glinted with black stars. "Larger than me." He took a step toward her and she held her ground. The heat of his body flowed into her as the mist fell upon him, licking and slithering over every curve and hollow. "My mother gave him many offspring. Each different from the last, and with her blood," his fingers lifted to curl into her hair, "and her magic," he tugged, prickling her scalp, "they quickly took over the tribe."

"So it can be done?" She raised her eyes to his, swaying lightly on her feet.

"Oh, yes. It can be done."

Her hair was suddenly yanked, tilting her face up to his and her mouth was captured. Her gasp of breath was lost between their lips. The kiss was hard, ungiving, a burst of force she wasn't ready for. He claimed her mouth, taking it as easily and as quickly as one of the willow growths. Aldora squeezed her eyes shut as his dark, beady gaze tried to capture more from her.

Vedikus. His name was a rattled curse in her head, a word spat and hissed out as he licked at her teeth, seeking to fill her up in every way possible. Aldora clutched his wrists and arched away, only to be wrangled closer to him until her body was pressed completely to his. She was consumed and taken over, a fate she neither wanted nor asked for but had been given into regardless of how much she tried to fight it.

Her captor was violent. Primal. His lips crushed and controlled hers relentlessly. The thick, flat, wet stab of his tongue explored her own, coaxing it into battle. A frustrated moan sounded from the back of her throat as she fought for a sliver of control.

This wasn't a kiss. It was power. The type that was addictive and sought after, the kind that dropped heroes to their knees. Her own grew weak.

His hand curved the back of her head and held her jittering body still, and every time she shifted, she brushed against his bulge. Aldora strained on her toes to keep her frame grounded, opening her eyes. In the back of her mind, she knew the moment he lifted her fully from the earth, she'd be nothing more than a receptacle for his dominion.

"Stop," she rasped, tearing her mouth to the side, his teeth scraping her lips. "Is that all you want from me?" His fingers pressed along her back, lifting her shirt up to knead her flesh. He made her muscles ache and then he made them melt under his touch.

He answered her with a snort and a jostle, jerking her body back up against his. His breath tickled her ears and she closed her eyes again with a shiver, her core coiling up with heat.

He frightens me.

Aldora clung to him as he pressed his hand lower, under the seam of her pants and toward the front where the tie loosened under his fingers. A chilly breath of air ghosted over the back of her legs as her pants slid to the ground to get caught in the dry stalks. Her undergarment rushed to meet them next, leaving her in nothing but her tunic and undershirt.

His mouth found hers again in a brutal kiss. She responded in turn, frustrated by his gorging, by his sudden lack of control, with the animalistic pawing and takeover of her body. Her feet arched, her joints stretched, trying to meet his demand and rise up on his body, but he kept her right on the precipice, right between being on the ground and fully within the power of his arms. Her nails bit into them as they raked up to grasp his shoulders. Her chest heaved as she gasped for air.

"You asked," he said, twisting his hand into her hair. "This is how it's done." He pulled her head back to pierce her with his eyes. They bore so deep within her head, her soul, that even if she lost the ability to see after this moment, the memory of them would forever be branded into her mind.

Her sex was barren and cold, exposed and open, her legs half hooked around his outer thighs as the flame of his hand pressed flat on her lower back; a warning. She could not look away from him despite the exposure. A breeze caressed her most intimate part, and she clenched around air, craving fulfillment.

His penetration.

Aldora tilted her head and watched him through her wisping hair, more nervous than she had ever been when it came to sex. *Since the moment I heard his voice...* She'd known, instinctively, he was already inside her then. *The moment I heard his voice and responded...*

Her core clenched again.

Vedikus is already inside me. His name had burrowed deep within and took root, intertwining with her own. *I want him there.*

A breathy, triumphant smile twisted his lips. Her sex throbbed, and she pressed herself forward instead of away.

"Aldora," he laughed low and deep, his voice milking more from her, making her forget the danger of their situation. "Are you trying to manipulate me?"

She hiked one leg up to hook over his hip and his hand moved down to cup her backside and lift her against him. "No," she breathed, believing it.

His sudden burst of dry laughter caught her off guard. The hand in her hair dropped out of sight, and suddenly she was shifted higher until she came to rest on top of his naked member. His engorged head thrummed with heat, and she tensed, realizing Vedikus had shed his loincloth. But it was his eyes holding her captive that kept her from fighting him, and the delicious tease of her core constricting as she felt his tip so close to where she ached. It slid through her folds, and his nostrils flared to release a stream of smoke.

"Mount me," he demanded, raising the hair on the back of her neck.

Aldora shivered and narrowed her eyes. He pressed his tip to her entrance.

"Mount me, female." This time his voice came out pained. His hands, rough on her skin, moved down to hold her just upon him. He seated her on his bulge, pressing into her but going no further. She squirmed from the burn and felt more wetness leak out of her in response.

His fingers moved to press and rub up and down her sex, slipping through her essence to widen and expose her sex even more.

"Don't…" he growled in the misty morning daylight, "make me ask again."

She was afraid to try and a whimper escaped her lips. Vedikus was giant compared to the men of her past. His gaze darkened upon her and a need to please him suddenly consumed her. She moved upon him slowly at first, then jerkily and the pleasure grew. He gripped her bruisingly and she thought he would impale her but as her movements slowed he loosened his hold slightly.

She moaned and clutched his bestial length, and forced herself on him. A soft cry escaped her lips that grew into breathy shrieks, her body stretching slowly, painstakingly over his hard flesh. She couldn't see what was happening, and he kept her from doing so, but she could *feel* everything.

This was different from feeling him inside her, imagining it from the beginning. She always knew there would be pain, pain from the intrusion, the invasion, the domination, but the delicious lick and burn she felt as she worked herself over him was something more. To be stared at so intensely, that she could not deny what he was, captivated her.

If he wants fear from me, it won't be from this.

Aldora slipped down his shaft with a mewling wail, squeezing her eyes shut as his hands pinched her flesh. Her body shook, but he held her upright and in the air as her hips quirked to gain more ground.

"I don't think I can," she cried out, twitching on his length, still only half-seated on it, her body opened as far as she could get it without his help. Her legs gripping his hips.

"You have no choice," he grunted, squeezing her again, but hefting her off his length and pressing her shaking form hard against his chest. "Now you know what you should prepare for," he growled. She wrapped her arms around him and held on, flinching from the sudden loss of him inside her and confused why he had allowed her to stop. Time passed as she caught her breath and the strain of her muscles eased. His shaft continued to twitch and seek her heat against her inner thigh. She waited for him to position her again, but as time continued to pass, she knew they were done.

But for how long? Her core clenched, seeking his intrusion, his burn, but it was gone. And only the ache of her brutal stretching remained.

Sweat formed on her brow, over her palms, making her skin slippery as she exhaled and lowered her legs to stand. His loincloth fell back into place.

Vedikus released her, and the mood shifted between them. Aldora peeled her hands off his flesh and brushed her fingers through her tangled hair, refusing to meet his eyes. Minutes before she was staring him down but now she couldn't muster the courage to look at him. In her periphery, steam continued to trail from his mouth and nose. Her body wouldn't stop shivering as she turned away and dressed.

His voice stopped her as she lifted her undergarment. "We will try again soon, female, do not bother layering yourself up."

Aldora gripped her pants.

I belong to him.

Chapter Twelve

Vedikus scanned his surroundings, searching the plains for a sign of Prayer. They had been walking for hours with nothing but shallow bog and high grasses to greet them in every direction.

He sucked in a breath, feeling the slick chill of the mist flood his senses. In all sense of the mist, it should have been untouchable, unfeelable, but it wasn't. It *could* be felt, and it *was* tangible. Like the steam his body released could be felt. The mist was like a vaporous poisonous gas so thick it whispered across your skin like a brush of feathers.

He never noticed it unless he fixated on it because the curse had been a constant in his life since the second he was birthed from his mother's womb. Even through the wet slop of his birth, he could feel the curse envelop him into a new, more horrid womb. One he would never be delivered from.

The rope tied about his waist tugged at his middle and he waited a moment for Aldora to catch up.

He only focused on the mist because of her. It grounded him enough to not strip her anew and have her mount him again.

I begged.

Vedikus sneered, palming the handle of his axe. His prick was as hard as ever, now coated with a human female's essence, and chafing against his leathers. It had been a distraction before, but now that he had sampled Aldora's hot quim, he was now deranged with an entirely new curse.

His body was primed to mate. And when a minotaur was primed, its true self came to light. Blood was shed, and scars were made. He had not expected to feel so desperate so quickly after capturing his her. He had not been prepared, and despite how much that agitated him, it was the truth. If anything should ambush them now, he would thank his gods for coming to his salvation.

His father had become the tribe's chief several years after he had brought back his mother from the border. She had arrived already pregnant with his eldest brother and free of the corruption, but what had happened to his mother and his sire between her capture and delivery was lost to him. Their couplings were often frenetic and public during his youth, but so were the mating habits of the rest of his old tribe. There was no shame in the act, but with Aldora...

Her skin pinkens, her voice hitches. She cannot mount me at will. He liked how she reacted. He liked the struggle. He liked it so much it made him throb and crave her more. His fingers danced over his weapon. *The way she shudders and moans.* It made the act heretical.

Vedikus cracked his neck.

He looked around. Nothing but eerie stillness and the ever-present buzzing of swamp bugs met him in every direction. In the daylight, all appeared deserted and settled here, but it was a trap to all outsiders. The moment the tiny ball of sun that shone through the mist began to descend, the bog would wake up like a gaping mouth stretched into a toothy yawn. He had traversed the lands around Prayer many times in his travels but rarely did he ever enter its grounds. It was protected with heavy wafts of dark magic that pulsated from its source: the settlement at its center. A place no one ventured despite its safety, because of how easy it would devour your soul.

Vedikus stilled as a breeze twitched his ears.

"Is something wrong?" Aldora asked quietly at his side.

He listened further but the wind was gone. "No." Vedikus glanced at her, his hooves slowly sinking into the muck. She had redressed herself despite his order, and the sudden need to tear her clothes to shreds quickly overcame him. She hid her mouth behind the back of her hand and her tongue darted out to swipe across it.

His eyes sharpened as she lifted her chin to meet his gaze. Her eyes widened, lips pursing, and the damning need to have her mount his body had him forgetting the real danger they were in. Vedikus tasted blood in his mouth, impure sanguine that teased at the purity just within reach.

She braces for me. His prick twitched uncomfortably. If she had been a half-breed like him, a female of his tribe, he would have had her under him in the grasses already, feeding his bulge between her thighs.

Vedikus could hear her heart begin to pound under his scrutiny. She pressed the back of her hand hard against her mouth.

"Why do you do that?" he asked, tense.

He watched as Aldora slowly comprehended his words and drew her hand away from her face to study it. The silence lingered and he flicked his tail. Vedikus reached out and tangled his fingers into her hair and forced Aldora to look at him. "What is wrong?"

"I couldn't taste the meat."

It took a moment for him to realize she meant the meat from earlier. He stiffened and drew her near. "You did not tell me?"

"I didn't know until I ate. I thought it was because I couldn't smell, that its taste was dulled, and the more I chewed, the more I realized it was me. I'm afraid of what will go next," she blurted out. "I keep licking my skin, hoping to taste sweat."

Had she lost two senses in that many days? *How is that possible?* "Have you lost anything else?" The need to get her the cure weighed down on him again and he cursed the distractions that had delayed them. Cursed his lust.

"N-no. Nothing else, not yet at least. Is it supposed to take effect this fast?" Aldora licked her hand again and he captured it afterward, sliding his tongue where hers had just been. *I taste salt and sweat, bitter and sweet.* The flavors burst over his tongue.

Vedikus raised his head and scanned the perimeter, peering as far as he could before the haze closed in on him. He glanced at the sun and knew they had not turned around or walked in circles. The mud was a clear indication that progress had been made. *This is why the wetlands around Prayer are so dangerous.* The more you wanted to reach your destination, the quicker the paranoia came to take over your mind. He checked again and closed his eyes. Aldora pulled her hand from his and wiped it on her tunic.

"No," he said after his initial unease left him, and with it his immediate need to mate. "It should take a moon cycle for it to weaken you enough to take your sense of self."

"I still feel like myself."

"And you have lost your ability to smell and taste." He grasped her arm and continued walking. "It should take longer than several days."

"Did it take longer for your mother?" she asked.

Vedikus stilled and thought back to the stories he had been told, then moved forward once again. Time chased them faster than the other labyrinthian creatures did. Their steps slurped with their speed.

"My mother was treated when she made it back to the tribe." He was sure of it. "They journeyed a fortnight prior. Most humans, if they live past the first night of entering here, are treated away from the walls. It's too dangerous otherwise. I wouldn't be taking you to Prayer if you weren't degrading so fast."

Faster still than he had thought.

Aldora matched his pace, and her long hair breezed over his arm. The touch did little to ease him. She brought her hand to her mouth again and he stopped her.

"Don't do that." Vedikus took it and held it firmly this time. "You'll just lick your skin off trying to seek something that is no longer there for you."

"It brings me comfort."

"Then it is a trick of the mind."

"Everything has been a trick here. I'm not supposed to be here!" He picked up his pace and pulled her after him despite the mud trying to slow them down. "I'm supposed to be on the farm," Aldora's voice had gone hollow, "tending to the apple trees and preparing deliveries. My father would be hauling the crates onto the cart while my mother spoke to the townsfolk. She and Mr. Branis would be arguing and the sickeningly sweet smell of fresh jam would be making me nauseous. I hated it..." Her tone deadened on a whisper. "I shouldn't be here."

Stopping short, Vedikus turned and faced her, forcing her to look at him. Her brown eyes were glazed over and his throat tightened, imagining her going blind. "Aldora," he warned. "I will have your thoughts." *She looks at me as if she doesn't see me.*

"I wish I was back home, with the apples, and their nauseating scent," she said quietly.

He did not know what she spoke of but knew, when her eyes did not focus on him, that she wasn't listening to his command. Aldora lowered her head and looked away, allowing her hair to fall before her face. He swiped the strands away. "Tell me about them."

"The apples?" she sniffled.

"Yes."

"They were the best in Thetras, the best in all the western regions of Savadon. They're bright and blood red with a gleam that reflected the midday sunlight. When polished for market, I could see my reflection mar their surface, a blight to their natural beauty. They filled my arms and when not watched carefully, would tumble and roll away."

They had nothing like that in these lands. "Do you speak of mountain rocks? Rubies?" he asked.

"No." Aldora focused on him. "They looked like rubies, the best ones of the yearly crop, but those were saved for the celebrations in the capital. Have you never seen an apple?"

"I've never heard of them."

"I can't believe that." She gripped his wrist and pulled his hand from her face. "They're a common crop. My mother's grove is right on the other side of the wall and stretches for a hundred acres."

"So, they are a grown food," he stated, thinking back. Vine bread was considered food given by the land if cooked correctly, and there were edible roots and herbs that could be found if one was looking, but not much else, and not something that looked like rubies.

"Yes, from apple trees. One tree can produce hundreds of them."

"Do they taste of blood?"

She frowned, her mouth parting in shock. "They're sweet and sour, enough so they make your teeth ache. Nothing like blood. Do you really not have apples?"

Vedikus straightened. "No." And they never would.

"Then…" she paused, "I'll never see one again, never eat one again."

"Most things that grow here are as hard and as horrid as the creatures that walk this land. If you ever see one of these apple trees appear in the mists, avoid it for they are an illusion to lure you closer."

"Then are you an illusion too?"

Vedikus stilled and peered down at her. "What do you think, female?"

"If you are, you're a painful one." She placed a hand carelessly on her chest and turned away. He clenched his fist to keep from reaching for her and forced himself to slowly relax it and settle back on his weapon.

"We are both painful illusions then," he muttered and continued walking.

Time passed by in silence with nothing but the sound of their footsteps, and after a short span, he found it grating. "Tell me more about these apples if they make you feel better," Vedikus heard himself saying.

"They don't make me feel better. They make me feel worse."

He grunted but let the subject drop.

The tall grass shortened into thick, short stalks the farther they trudged, and his hooves began to stick in the muck. Each moment the land pulled at them from below as if hungry for their energy, and his unease built with every step. Aldora's gasping pants grew labored as he pushed them forward, but she kept up and remained at his side with no complaint to accompany them. Her determination was equal to his own.

Prayer had the means to cure a human but it also had the means to further curse them. It depended entirely on what its protector demanded of them. He had little on himself to offer for payment. But the longer he listened to his female laboring at his side, he knew that whatever the hag asked of him, he would give it.

Aldora had been forced to sacrifice her life to end up

by his side, and if the human could do that—without once giving up—he could do more.

I will do whatever I can to get her to my brothers alive. He wouldn't have been hunting along the border if it weren't for his tribe. For the longevity and the future that he and his brothers were so determined to have. It had been years since he had last seen the bulls of his father's tribe, years since he felt the comfort of stability.

He looked up at where the mist shrouded the horizon and pictured the mountains looming just beyond his sight. They were not far from where the Bathyr waited, and once they made their way out of the bog, it would only be a matter of days before he had delivered his breeder safely to their camp.

The mountain pass and crevasses would be guarded by a thousand traps and watched over by his brothers Dezetus, Hinekur, and Thyrius. Nothing had been able to traverse it since they claimed the land, and nothing ever will now that they had a human to protect.

After they had abandoned the old tribe, he and his brothers had left the dead lands—the lands far from all human civilization—and made their way back to the barrier lands, where true power was tested. It was dangerous to live so close to the human world of Savadon but it was the only way for him and his brothers to survive and build their own tribe. Humans did not appear randomly deep within the world, and fresh blood was a perpetual need.

My offspring will be strong. Aldora's hair breezed across his arm and his tail lashed impatiently.

Suddenly, a dull green light flashed at the edge of their

bubble, extinguishing the tension that threatened to burst from his bones. Vedikus approached the gaseous light. *About time.*

"What is that?" The female wheezed, breathless at his side.

"That is our pathway into Prayer."

"Vedikus!"

He didn't hear the whiz of the spear until it was too late.

Chapter Thirteen

Aldora saw the outline of a dozen centaurs as she caught sight of the green light. One moment there had been nothing but mist, and in the next, it was broken up to reveal a pack of them with weapons poised. She screamed Vedikus's name as they raised their weapons to attack.

Several spears sliced the air, cutting through the swirling, ethereal fog.

Her heart stopped as a spray of blood splattered the grass, accompanied by a howl. Vedikus dropped to his knees and she ran forward to reach him, her eyes trained on nothing but him and the burst of red gushing from his wounds. Her fingers found his when something caught her from behind, lifting her away.

"No!" she screamed. She fought whoever held her as she was swooped away by a pair of arms, kicking out and grasping for something—anything—within reach to fight her attacker. But her strength was nothing compared to a centaur and she was swiftly carried to the other side of the clearing.

"Your time has come Minotaur," one of them shouted as they moved in to surround him.

"Vedikus!" she shrieked, seeing him rise up with his axes dripping with his blood. His flesh was torn from where several spears had grazed him. He glanced her way, rage filling his eyes and for a moment in time the mists surrounding him swirled across his body and illuminated his frame. He took a step toward her.

The centaurs closed in with sharp lances.

Panic laced her veins and her throat tightened, as a gut-wrenching wail rose from her chest. It was muffled when a palm covered her mouth.

"Calm, little human, calm," a man hummed softly in her ear, holding her tightly against his unfamiliar body. She was held like a ragdoll, subdued with her feet swinging above the ground, higher up than any mere man could hold her. Realization struck her as bloodcurdling roars pierced her ears, that she was being trotted away. The ground moved swiftly beneath her dangling feet. "Calm, calm."

Aldora tensed her fingers, reaching whatever flesh she could of her abductor to tear with little leeway. *I need to get to the ground.*

The yells raised and faded with each clash of metal, growing more distant each second. Tears pricked her eyes as she imagined the razor bone tips of the spears stabbing Vedikus's body again and again. Her nails tore deep when she found velvet hide.

"Calm!" the centaur hissed, jostling her.

She didn't care what he had to say and pressed the soles of her boots against his front legs and pushed off with all her might. Sweaty hands slid across her skin and she began to drop. They caught on her clothes before falling away completely, ripping the sleeve of her tunic.

She fell forward and landed hard on her knees, her arms slamming into the sodden ground a moment too late to catch her fall.

"Feral female," the centaur sneered, rounding to her side, "we are here to save you, not hurt you!"

Aldora bit through the pain and grasped her dagger, rising up to face her new abductor, intent on killing him. *I need to get back to Vedikus.* His name rose up like a mantra in her head. *Vedikus.* It cleared the chaos in her mind.

The centaur trotted in a circle around her, just out of her reach. One of his hands pressed against his side where she'd scratched it. Her fingers slipped across the smooth handle of her weapon, half-hidden in the grasses. Her calves quivered within the dampening cloth of her pants, soaking up the bog water.

"You *are* hurting me," she rasped, eyes following the centaur as he continued to circle her. She moved with him to keep him in her sight.

"You did that to yourself. You have spent too long in the minotaur's company."

"It was not by choice. It is now."

The centaur crept closer and she dropped back. *Stay outside of his reach.* If she had learned anything from her childhood, it was to stay outside the reach of an animal, farm or otherwise. One misplaced kick could drop you if not kill you.

"Is it? Little of us are given the freedom to choose, and those that do…" The centaur looked behind her to where the others had disappeared. "Some kill and ask questions later."

Aldora's lips flattened. It was what she'd planned to do.

"Some? No one has remained alive in his presence, nor mine since I was tossed into your world. I saw your kind several nights ago in the fray killing all who neared."

"Yes, we were there, the leader of our herd, myself, and Telner." The centaur's voice lowered. "We fought to keep you alive."

"And Vedikus," she added, taking a short step away. "He kept me alive."

His eyes narrowed. "The minotaur will pay for stealing you away."

"Why didn't you attack him like you had the rest? Why wait until now when you had the chance then?" Her eyes roved over the creature idly staring at her with interest. He was the first centaur she had seen clearly. The others had been a blur in the mist. His hair was long like a woman's and woven into a myriad of braids over his shoulders and back; they sparkled when slivers of light made its way through the gloom and made a dull *clink* when he tossed his head.

Nothing sparkled here, and the tiny glints looked so unlike the horrible, shrouded, monotony of colors that made up the rest of this world.

"Did you not see the creatures that had come to take you? Those who would rape and eat you?"

"I can't see in the dark," she snapped, still circling with him.

The noises in the distance suddenly stopped. Aldora clenched her dagger and strained to hear, hoping that Vedikus's voice would call out to her. The centaur whistled and was met with another that approached, and in the distance, a quick pounding of hooves from a dozen horsemen running through the mud met her ears.

"You heard them then," the centaur said smugly.

I hear them now.

She twitched to run, to slink into the fog and escape. She saw herself, breathless, sprinting through the grasses, drenched in sweat and gray water, searching for Vedikus. But there was nothing except the sound of pursuit. The panic, the racing of her blood, and the ache of her body going toward nowhere with only a breathy prayer on her lips. It flashed in her head, her boots weighed down with mud and water. The decision to *try* wavered.

Would they leave Vedikus behind to bleed out, or capture him like they captured her? Would they take her to Prayer?

Do they know I'm sick? There was no place to hide.

The centaur reached out his hand to help her straighten from where she crouched. She eyed the outstretched hand, pale and rough with long fingers and thick knuckles, partially hidden by worn leather stretched across its back. So human, so normal.

Aldora swallowed and refused it, rising on her own to face him.

She lowered her weapon as he dropped his hand, regarding her with an expression she couldn't read. The centaur whistled again, and within the next moment, she was surrounded by a group of horsemen that towered over her from every side. She hugged herself and searched for Vedikus among them—hoping they had taken him prisoner—but he was not there. She kept looking.

"You're safe now, female," said a new speaker, a centaur with blood-stained bandages draped across his naked chest. He stepped forward. Her gaze dragged over him for a moment but continued on past him to look at the mist beyond, waiting for Vedikus to spring forward.

He did not.

Vedikus.

The thought of his name gave her strength.

Aldora.

His eyes snapped open.

Vedikus groaned, staring up at the sky. It was duller than before, and he could no longer see the tiny dot of the sun. He had lost consciousness and was weaker than he was before, but heard the splash of hooves moving farther away.

Where is she? Nothing but pearly mist met him in every direction. It had all happened so quickly—the ambush—and he had been too distracted to see the signs.

The centaurs had left him alive, if barely, but he knew if he rested until his wounds closed, he would be dead long before midnight.

He sucked in a shuddering breath.

Vedikus pulled himself upright and peered down at the damage that had been done to him.

His chest and gut had been stabbed through several

times, and there were gashes on his arms along with several smaller ones on his legs. Blood leaked from each of them to the ground below where it was diluted by the tepid water. He placed his weight on his palms and straightened his upper half out of the muck. *A red boil, burst open. A pool of my own waste.*

Not just mine. There were two dead centaurs a short distance from him. Their bodies added to the stench of gore that permeated around him. He'd been so focused on Aldora that he had let them surround him, had given them the advantage.

He gritted his teeth as another wave of agony coursed through him.

The green light that heralded the entrance to Prayer twinkled in his peripheral vision, barely discernible without Aldora's blood clearing the way. He'd grown used to it as he stared at the glimmer; the clarity, the colors, the extra light reaching through from overhead. She was better than any magic or drug.

He immediately missed her comforting presence, her smell, her defiance, and her submission. Knowing she may well still be alive was enough to bear the pain. She was his. HIS. If they touched her, he would make sure every last centaur in the land died horribly. They had already taken her from him and that was enough to solidify their deaths.

Vedikus surged to his hooves. Blood and water poured from his wounds. When nothing attacked him, he waited several minutes in silence and took in his surroundings.

The grasses had all been trampled upon, and those that weren't were splattered with gore. The corpses nearby had been looted of their weapons but nothing else. He looked for his own but could not find them, feeling the loss of their weight at once.

Vedikus pressed his hand over the wound in his gut but knew it would do little to help. It was deep, and he knew it to be beyond his ability to heal with the supplies he had on hand.

Vengeance would strengthen him.

He made his way over to one of the corpses. He kneeled before one, wondering why the rest of the pack had left their dead behind.

The Bathyr honored their dead.

Vedikus tore off the corpses armor, ripping the cloth he found into strips for bandages and bowed his head. He gave them their last rites and wished them an eternity of failure in the afterlife.

Chapter Fourteen

The centaurs made camp after thrusting one of their spears into the ground and binding her to it. They took her dagger and the bandaged one checked her for others, running his splayed hands all over her body. The others watched it happen with intense expressions. Their cocks jutted, dripping with cum from their bodies.

Aldora shut her eyes.

When he was done, she swallowed the blood in her mouth from where her teeth had sunk into her tongue. Aldora observed the centaurs quietly as they unloaded packs and sheathed their weapons. She tried to be discreet in pulling out the spear that bound her, but the mud refused to relinquish it. So she worked on dislodging it bit by bit, pretending to shiver from the evening breeze.

They watched her back.

It was still day when several of them placed large clusters of wood onto the ground. She couldn't figure out where they had gotten it. But the wood was erected in a wide circle around her and lit, bursting from embers to flames. Within minutes the chill of the wetlands was entirely replaced with heat. One of the centaurs sprinkled something into the fires that made them grow until they were large enough to engulf entire trees.

They chanted words into the flames that she did not know while the one with bandages continued to watch her. He made her the most nervous out of them all.

She wasn't ready when he approached her.

"I can move you now," he said, coming to a stop at her side. "If you're cold. The fires will help dry your skin and draw the moisture within the ground. You do not have to stay where it is wet."

"I'm not cold." She quickly suppressed her fake shivers, not wanting to be touched by him again. "Did you kill him?" she asked, her throat tight.

The centaur canted his head. "Does it matter?"

"Yes," she snapped.

He went silent for a moment. "The minotaur has fallen, and if he has not yet died, he will soon. Do not worry, human, he will not hurt you anymore."

Aldora pursed her lips. The thought of Vedikus lying in the muck, bleeding out from his wounds, clinging to life, haunted her. He was there because of her. *But I'm here because of him.* She'd grown used to him, had come to rely on him in the short time they'd been together and now, as she watched the centaurs, she wished she was back by his side. She missed his overwhelming presence and wanted it back.

"Can you take me to him?"

"Are you looking for proof?"

What to say? She knew little about what these new men wanted with her, from her. If their cocks were any indication, it wasn't something good.

What if I ask for proof and they bring me back his head? They hadn't touched her since they took her weapon but they all stared at her with a fierceness that frightened her. *They watch me now.*

Aldora shook her head. "When is nightfall?" she asked instead.

"Several short hours away."

She had that much time to get to him. "Then why stay here?" *Vedikus never stopped unless he had to.*

The centaur raised a hand to his chest and ran it across his bandage. "The wounded need time to heal, to cauterize their skin and prevent further damage. This place is a bad place to bleed." He ran his eyes over her body. "I see you have wounds that require healing yourself." He reached for her and she shrunk back.

"Are you afraid of me?" he asked.

"I don't know you."

"Would you like to know me?"

"No."

Several of the centaurs laughed, but the bandaged one's face hardened.

Aldora chewed on her lip realizing her mistake. If she angered him what would he do to her then? "What are you going to do to me?" She slowly moved her eyes down from his face and to his front hooves, taking stock of his weapons. *Two spears. A shortsword. A bow and quiver. And my dagger.* Aldora itched to wrap her fingers around it again.

The hardness of his features eased. "That depends on

you." The centaur shook his head, rattling her ears with more clinks. But then he moved away. He picked up a discarded spear and began to sharpen it near one of the fires feverishly. Their eyes met through the flames and she quickly looked away.

What can I do?

The centaurs convened in small groups around her, weaving in and out of the three bonfires they had erected. Several of them lit their spears on fire and used them as torches. Whatever they were made of repelled the flame and kept them from burning up. Aldora felt around the spear at her back wondering if it were fireproof too. It was smooth and cold to the touch, and when she wrapped her fingers around the shaft and pulled, it still wouldn't move.

It bode ill for whether or not she could even wield it. She had nothing else on or near her that she could find that would be able to help her. She dropped her fingers from the spear and returned her attention to the encampment.

What would Vedikus do if he was in her place? A self-deprecating laugh left her lips, bringing all eyes back to her, reminding her of how exposed she was. Her gaze lowered to her torn, damp clothes. They clung to her and left little to the imagination, and even with her undergarments still intact, her nipples poked through from the abrasion.

She could still feel the ache between her thighs where Vedikus had worked his cock into her, forcing her body to stretch and take it. She flushed and squeezed her legs together, feeling even more vulnerable under so many intense stares.

She had noticed the centaur's pricks remained erect,

much how Vedikus' had at the beginning. Her eyes were drawn to that area despite the fear they made her feel. Was it because she was surrounded and that they all displayed hunger in their eyes? Or was it the sudden threat they posed that made her stiff and wary? These men were half human, half horse, just as Vedikus was spliced with his own beast, and like all beasts, they were well endowed.

An idea came to mind, and a very real shiver came with it.

Aldora moved to sit on her knees and met the eyes of the bandaged one again. "I'd like to be closer to the fire," she whispered, unable to make her voice rise. He seemed to hear her though. The centaur stabbed his spear into the ground and came back to her side. In one quick move, he yanked out the stake that bound her to the ground, reaching his other hand out to grasp her arm and help her to her feet.

She bit down on her tongue and focused on the pain as she accepted the touch and was led away from the middle, immediately feeling better now that she wasn't so fully encircled. Aldora slunk to the ground by one of the bonfires, surprised to find the dirt and grass dry.

"What's your name, human?"

"Aldora."

"What does it stand for?"

She frowned and looked down at her hands. "It stands for nothing."

He whinnied and moved into her line of sight. "Then it stands for you, a survivor of the barrier paths, a rescued human, and a killer of bulls."

Her gaze snapped up, narrowing. "I haven't killed anything."

"You may not have held the blade but we have decided to gift you with the minotaur's death, our gift to you for being alive when we found you."

Her frown deepened and she glanced briefly at the other centaurs. *I don't understand.* She had lived next to this world her entire life. Why had there been so little knowledge of what happened within? There were survivors that made it out and her mind lingered on them, disturbed why Savadon and its authority took their accounts with distrust.

Savadon should have been preparing to fight those that frightened them, that had taken away their land, but instead, her people had tried to appease the mist.

"Thank you," she muttered.

"For what?"

"The gift." She breathed in deeply before asking. "Will you give me another?"

The centaur smiled slowly and she looked away. "We are bargainers after all. My name is Alepos, what do you seek from me and my men?"

To deliver me to Vedikus and to leave us alone! She licked her lips. Was that what she really wanted? Aldora studied the flames and watched them lick the air. "W-will you unbind my hands?"

The centaur went silent. And the longer it lasted the harder it was for her to remain upright. She began to feel what courage she had left leave her when he finally spoke.

"And what would you offer us in return?"

"Whatever it is that you want from me," she lied but noticed several of the centaurs pause. *It doesn't matter.*

Aldora shuffled to her feet and turned, stretching out her arms, waiting for one of them to loosen the binds. She did not look up to see which centaur cut her free, but instead brought her wrists to her chest and rubbed them.

And rubbed them.

And continued to do so as she sank back down to her knees, facing the fire. Alepos brought her food but it went uneaten at her side.

The sun was lost in the smoke when the first swell of her blood appeared beneath her nails. Her skin was raw and red as she dug into it faster, spurred on by the blood. She let her head drop to hide what she was doing with her hair. The centaurs continued to watch her but she faced away from them and toward the fire. Several came by to speak to her, but she didn't hear any of it as she raced the encroaching darkness.

Her nail snagged where she had broken the skin and, wincing from the pain, she worked it open until her hand came away wet with blood. It flowed red-hot over her skin and pooled into her lap where her pants soaked it up. Aldora gritted her teeth and quickened her speed, scratching even harder now, uncaring of who saw.

A nearby shriek assailed the encampment just as the centaurs yelled her way. It heightened to an ear-piercing level that was soon followed by a dozen other similar shrieks in the distance.

Aldora widened her eyes and looked up disbelieving that her plan had worked.

"What have you done!?" She was wrenched to her feet. Furious eyes bore down on her as her bleeding arm was lifted for all to see. A responding roar went out as spears were lifted off the ground.

Alepos dropped her arm with a hiss, but it was already too late.

Aldora smiled. The smell of her blood was in the evening air.

Vedikus lurked within the reeds and smelled his way toward the fire. The air was thick with it. Thick with revenge. Thick with his need.

The armor and cloth he'd looted from the corpses chafed his skin where he'd used it to bind his wounds, hoping he'd be alive long enough to stitch them back together. It would take more than a stab in the gut to stop him; his organs were tougher than that.

But none of that would matter if he lost Aldora. *She can't get away.* The thought alone made him want to go berserk. His vision blurred as he imagined grabbing the centaurs' heads and crushing them between his palms. He could almost feel their bones cracking beneath his hands. He grabbed a clump of grass and ripped it from the ground. The centaurs would die. They would die tonight.

The fires rose before him, brilliant against the grey gloom of the bog, and his eyes watered despite being well outside the camp. They smelled bitter, releasing the fragrance of blisterwood with strong undertones of enios sea salt which repelled all but the hungriest of undead and was only found within centaur lands. *I am not dead yet.*

Vedikus pressed a hand to his stomach but it came away wet with blood—a lot of blood.

He had packed the wound with whatever herbs he had left—whatever he hadn't eaten—but it hadn't been enough to staunch the flow of fully numb his pain. There had been nothing left over for his other wounds.

None of it matters if Aldora is dead.

His gaze landed on her, a small husk bent over by the fire nearest to where he hid. *Look at me.* Vedikus willed it, uncaring if it gave him away. *Look for me.* Her head lifted and her hair fell back to reveal an ashen, pained expression flickering between a wince and determination. He squinted his eyes and focused on her, discerning what caused her such discomfort. Her eyes never found him despite his internal plea, and a breath of steam released from his mouth.

He wanted her to see him, hoped that it would bring her some sort of comfort that he was alive and watching, but repressed a laugh at his absurdity. *Just because she's mine doesn't mean she cares for me.*

He frowned as the chief centaur made his way to her side with food. Vedikus tensed to charge forward and ram his horns into the male for daring to offer his female anything without his permission. The meal went ignored at her side and slowly his rage lessened. Alepos left tersely to help his fellow studs cauterize their flesh.

Their groans and hisses pleased him.

Aldora dropped her head and he could no longer see her face. He slunk back and lowered himself into the mud.

There were ten centaurs in the camp that he could count, with the possibility of at least a half-dozen more scouting outside his view. *I killed two.* And he would have killed more if he hadn't become so distracted with his need for the female.

Vedikus cursed under his breath.

The centaurs remained on alert but he could easily tell they had become just as focused on Aldora as he had been, as he tried not to be now.

She was beautiful. He hadn't realized it until he almost lost her, but seeing her again, alive, if hurt, made him want to claim her in full view of the others. Despite his rent skin, despite the pain, he would take her in the center of the bonfires where the flames would roar in his ears, her moans ringing out, and her body riding his. *Let the studs see what they'll never have.*

But first, he needed a distraction or a temporary ally. He scanned the vicinity already knowing he would have no aid, and he would never be able to leave for fear Aldora would be gone or dead when he made it back. Rallying at Prayer was out of the question.

The undead that rose from the swamps would not help him due to the fires.

His axes were gone. Vedikus found the *horse* that had looted them and sneered, his nostrils flaring wide. He clenched his hands before calming himself. Even equipped with a superior weapon, the centaur would kneel before him and beg for death.

Tactics and sneak attacks were not his strength, and stealth was all but out of the question. His brother, Astegur, was the planner, the wily one of the Bathyr whose war cry was known far and wide as a signal of a trap having been sprung. Vedikus had never envied the skills of one of his brothers so much as he did now. He could not take a band of centaurs on dry, open lands. Their advantage was too great on prepared terrain.

Come darkness, I'll use the fire.

I'll light the reeds, and the grasses, the small critters, and set the plains on fire. He could see it in his skull and he grabbed another cluster of stalks and ripped them from the earth. He released a hot exhale of steam over them to dry them out.

Something ripe tickled his nose, just under the sea salt and smoke. It pulled him out of his thoughts. He turned his face up to catch more of the scent.

Aldora.

He caught it, knew it, just as a sudden gust of wind took it from him and blew it away. Vedikus tensed, his eyes searching for her among the camp. She had not moved but her arms shook and her body twitched. She was doing something to herself within the curtain of her hair.

Several of the studs stilled and eased up from the ground, and he knew… There would be no plan tonight.

Only death to those who have tried to come between him and Aldora.

A screeching, ear-piercing howl filled his ears and he rose to his feet, his hooves sinking deep into the mud. The smell of pure human blood on the wind was enough to wake any slumbering creature and drive them into a frenzy.

Alepos rushed toward Aldora, and it was the last clear thing he saw be a red haze descended over his mind.

Chapter Fifteen

Aldora was dropped violently to the ground by the centaur as something crashed into his side. A battle roar joined the approaching barks of barghests in the distance. She scurried back on her hands and feet and moved away from the scene.

"Ready your spears—" Alepos's command suddenly cut off.

She glanced back to see his body kicking and seizing on his side within the bonfire. Bile rose in her throat as his pained screams filled the air. It wasn't the centaur flailing in the fire that stopped her from fleeing but the horned minotaur atop him, clutching his skull.

"Vedikus!" Aldora screamed, watching the flames lick his sides. She startled as centaurs closed in on Vedikus from every side. "Watch out!"

She dodged away from the horsemen approaching her and moved around the bonfire. Two circled to either side to trap her when a steady, low vibration filtered through the space, over her skin, and into her bones. The howls had vanished and she stilled, swallowing, as the centaur closest to her stopped and slowly raised his spear.

"Behind you, female. Do not move," he rasped out, leaving his back open. Her eyes skirted to the other centaur who was also lifting his weapon and looking at something past her.

The vibration built throughout her whole body and her skin turned to gooseflesh. Aldora could feel something behind her, could sense it through its ravenous aura. There was nothing to protect her if the barghest pounced.

One by one the centaurs turned their attention to the creatures prowling outside the camp, the ones she had lured with her blood.

Please. Aldora screamed the word in her head. The growls deepened.

Her eyes found Vedikus rising out of the fire like an avenging demon, stepping over Alepos's charred corpse to meet his next opponent heading in her direction. The abrupt loss of their chief seemed to disorient the warriors. She hugged her arms, eyes widening as the fire lapped at Vedikus's hooves.

Relief surged through her and something more…

Something akin to awed terror at the monster that she'd come to rely upon, a thrilling, throat-constricting fear. A vengeful god.

"Duck!" the centaur closest to her screamed, startling her. He thrust his weapon as she dropped to the ground, the spear tip nearly catching her hair as Vedikus fought his way toward them. The two studs charged, and she huddled as they met the barghest head on. Their snarls and yells filled her ears. Unable to stay, she crawled toward the nearest fire before getting back to her feet.

Wherever she looked there were large black shadows attacking from every direction with giant jaws snapping as they dove from the dark mists and into the firelight. The barghests all aimed for her, their snouts twitching, breathing in the smell of smoke, cooked horse meat, and blood.

Another centaur charged across the clearing, stabbing his spear straight through the back of one of the monsters on his way toward her. She swiveled to the side and evaded his grasping arms, running toward Alepos's corpse.

"Aldora!" Vedikus called out to her, his voice a snarling rasp, no less wild than the growls of the barghests. "Come to me!"

She made it to the edge of the bonfire and skidded to a halt, bringing her hand to her mouth. A gag caught in her throat, followed by several more as she fought to contain them. Alepos was nothing more than a crackling husk of red and black meat, his clothing burned off with strands of hair flowing up with the smoke. His head was a ruined mess from Vedikus's iron grip, and she kneeled with her hand on her belly, applying pressure where her nausea grew. Aldora thanked the sun that she couldn't smell him or taste the smoke that filled her mouth.

With the cacophony of fighting filling her ears, she tore off the rest of her tunic sleeve and wrapped it around her hand. She reached for her weapon, which was still lying among the guttering flames. The flames lapped into the space but quickly weakened, although the wafting heat brought tears to her eyes.

Aldora grabbed her dagger and dropped it in the dirt before her knees. Rising quickly, she rolled it with her boot to cool it down.

She turned to seek out Vedikus when something clutched her hair and tugged her to her feet. She yelped and swung her blade, twisting around, and was caught mid-strike. Black, wild eyes met hers. Her gaze lifted to the blood-splattered horns above. "Vedikus." The air fled her lungs.

"Let's go," he said, releasing her hair. He was covered in soaked-through ragged bandages that fell off his muscles in wet ribbons. He had recovered both of his axes.

"We have to stay within the light," she gasped as he brought her to the camp's border, away from where the remaining centaur poked at the monsters skulking on the fringes of the campsite. Several more emerged from the mist as they entered the clear area around her. Vedikus let go of her and took up both axes again, hands crusted over with drying blood. Her own were dampened with sweat.

"The light won't last the night. I've fought more barghests than all the times the sun has shown through the mist. We can run to Prayer. Once we're within the circle of lights, we'll be safe."

"Your wounds…" They were apparent, even those that were covered, and she couldn't help but notice his pallid, pale complexion under the grime. His stance sagged between breaths and his head hung as if it was too hard for him to hold it up. *Have I made a mistake?*

"They are nothing," he snapped. Aldora grabbed his arm. "Can you run?"

She glanced down at herself, jerking when a scream

sounded from behind. She turned to see a centaur being dragged, horse legs kicking, by the jowls of a barghest deeper into the mist.

"I can run," she said quickly but eyed the others of the pack. They seemed to be waiting for her to do so. "Is there no other way?"

"Can you afford to lose more blood?" His question caught her off guard.

"I—" She stopped and hugged her clawed arm where most of the blood had stopped dripping. "I can lose more." She hadn't dug deep enough to lose a lot despite her efforts.

"Hand me your dagger." He turned toward her.

Aldora studied his face, trying to read it and find the strength she usually saw in his expression. She handed him the blade, still warm from the fire. It slipped from her fingers to his with her stomach in her throat.

"You'll need to trust me," Vedikus said.

She licked her lips. Vedikus took her hand that still had her sleeve wrapped around it and peeled it off. He raised the blade of the dagger to her palm and held her hand tight within his grasp. She braced herself for the pain she knew would come, barely aware of the fighting going on around them and the creatures that wanted to eat her. Aldora closed her eyes and gave herself up to what he wanted, but the blade paused, as if awaiting something from her. *I can take it.* She gritted her teeth and nodded.

It sliced across her flesh and an agonized moan rose from her throat. Just as swiftly, the cloth was back, soaking up her blood, and the howls rose back up from the ranks of the barghests. She flinched when Vedikus pulled back the cloth and replaced it with mud from below, caking her hand and wrist. The dirt filled her wound, and a stinging sensation replaced the heat.

The creatures surged in renewed frenzy, braving the firelight and rushing toward her. She was pulled hard into Vedikus's chest, and for a moment, the thundering of his heart matched her own and overtook all else. He threw the bunched up cloth across the clearing and howls intensified.

"Run!" Vedikus commanded.

She wasn't ready for it but had no choice as she was dragged back into the mist. It opened up as they sped through. The golden light from the bonfires vanished, and a rapidly darkening swamp met them on every side. She tripped, but Vedikus caught her, keeping her upright as they fled from the carnage, and the stifling heat quickly replaced with a humid chill as the mists pressed inwards. An uncomfortable hug that reminded her of a cold corpse.

Her lungs spasmed with pain, and murky water clung to her boots, making each step heavier than the last, but she kept going despite the ache, her wrist clutched in Vedikus's hold. The sound of barghests in pursuit followed.

They stopped suddenly and she was thrown to the ground just as something whipped past her head. She saw Vedikus whirl and slam the blade of his axe right into the barghest's head, filling her ears with a wet thump. Another one pounced as the first lay dying feet away. The second dropped immediately after, twitching next to the first when more appeared. One by one bodies fell around her and she jerked away, their snapping jaws still after her flesh even at the moment of death.

"We need to keep running," she yelled, bringing

Vedikus's attention back to her and away from the current body he was hacking. He rounded on her and offered his hand. She grabbed it and they took off with more beasts snapping at their heels.

Green lights appeared before her and she aimed for them through the tears in her eyes. *Make it. Please make it.* She lost her hold on the minotaur as she pumped her arms, fighting the air, the muck under her feet, and her screaming muscles. The first light blurred past her and she kept going. She pushed on until the howls lessened and were replaced by dying squeals.

Vedikus was no longer beside her.

Aldora fell to her knees and shook, feeling the frenzy burst through her and release with every gasp of breath. Sweat streamed from every pore. When she lifted her gaze, Vedikus was approaching her from the mist, axes dripping with gore. His eyes were on her in the same way he looked at an enemy.

She lowered her gaze just as his caked hooves entered her line of sight.

"I'm sorry," she whispered, still breathless.

A hand gripped her chin and raised it, tilting her to face up to him again. "As am I." He took her wounded hand and brought her palm to his mouth. His intensity pinned her as he licked the cut clean.

Chapter Sixteen

They made their way into Prayer, exhausted, dirty, and determined, following the eerie lights that led them to it. Somewhere in the darkening hours prior she had lost what was left of her reserve, and a riveting, guiltless freedom had taken its place. The sheer volume of blood she had seen was staggering: barghest, centaur, minotaur and her own. Spending so much time a moment away from death had changed her, and she didn't know if it was for the better or not. Regardless, she was alive, Vedikus was alive, and at that moment, nothing else mattered.

I'm alive.

Aldora rubbed her chest while half-stumbling under Vedikus's weight.

He leaned into her every now and then, head bowed and weakened. She wrapped her arm under his shoulder and tried to lend him some of her strength. *I've been using yours for too long.*

Before long, the lights expanded into a cluster in the

distance, and she could see the outlines of huts. They grew in size with each step forward to reveal crude symbols painted with a brown sludge over rotting wood. Beings moved within their haphazard wooden logs.

"Are you sure it's safe here?" she asked under her breath.

"No."

Aldora tensed under his arm. No one came out to greet them, but she knew they were there. Whatever they were. She could sense them and wasn't sure *why*, but they were nothing more than an obstacle in her mind. As long as they stayed away, she could pretend they weren't there.

The mud turned to dirt under her boots and after a short time of walking through the outskirts of the haven, she and Vedikus were trudging over rotten pallets risen slightly above the ground. They creaked and groaned with each step, some giving way under the minotaur's bulk.

They had made it to the center of the settlement, and she stopped before a stone building that looked more like a temple in Savadon than it did a structure set in the middle of a swamp. Vedikus breathed heavily at her side and she worried that he'd toppled against her at the building's steps. As they continued, she was unable to hold him upright, and he went down at her feet into a kneeling position with his horns pointed toward the dirt, his breaths growing heavier with each inhale.

Aldora grasped his shoulders and moved her hands up to cup his face, lifting it. "Vedikus," she strained before her voice went hard. "Get up." He was cold under her touch and had gone deathly pale. "You need to get up now. We made it after everything you've put me through—us through—if you leave me now…"

His beady black eyes stared back at her through a wet glare. Old and new blood coated him, and when she let go of his face, her hands came away coated with it.

"Get up," she snapped, feeling faint herself. A slow smirk spread across his lips, and she couldn't help but smile back with relief.

"You've brought me a gift."

Aldora tensed, her eyes trailing away from Vedikus as she turned to see who spoke at her back. She moved to shield him from whatever adversary might strike next. She felt him stand, shakily, using her shoulder as leverage behind her. She reached for her weapon when a young childlike woman covered in brown rags stepped from the shadows of the temple.

Her hand stilled at her side. The girl moved toward her, stopping a short distance away, just out of reach. She wore a sullen expression that bordered indifference and looked far too old to belong to her face. Aldora was at a loss to the girl's real age, and despite her appearance, she didn't seem entirely human.

But there's a girl, standing before me, alive, in the middle of this horrid place. Her mouth watered with questions.

"Do not trust her appearance," Vedikus breathed in her ear before she felt him lean slightly against her back.

"A gift?" the girl asked, glancing from her to Vedikus and back again.

Aldora shook her head. "We need your help."

"You need a cure."

"Yes. And sanctuary," Aldora amended.

"You brought a group of warrior centaur studs to my border, then a pack of barghests to sow chaos for your escape. I do not like chaos so close to Prayer, human," the girl spat. Aldora opened her mouth to ask her how she knew, but the girl continued. "Bring your human breeder inside, Minotaur, and make it quick before I decide that the price of your inconvenience is your lives." Without waiting, the girl walked back into the chilly recesses of the temple and disappeared within.

Aldora bristled, feeling her hope waver, but slid her arm around Vedikus, shaking under his weight.

Her gaze had adjusted to the darkness right as the stone walls glowed with the same pale green light from outside. She followed them to a nearly empty room with shriveled, long-dead vines hanging from the stone ceiling, and a sunken pool that took up half the floor. The water within was the same as the water from outside: murky with algae around the random thick stalks of grass that shot up from below. The only difference was it appeared deep and undisturbed.

There was a folded cloth next to it, and a charred pile of wood.

The girl was nowhere to be seen.

Aldora staggered to the edge of the bath, uncaring where the hag was and helped Vedikus sit. His hooves scraped across the floor. She took the offered towel and dipped it into the water, using it to clean both of them.

The dirt sloshed off their bodies in rivulets to seep back into the pool.

She brought her still-bleeding hand to his lips and he licked at it without speaking. A ticklish shiver shot through her. Her body reacted more for him than it ever had for a human man. She was beginning to like the power it lent her.

"Thank you," he grunted, strength and life returning to his voice.

She frowned. "You're not a thankful being."

"Even bulls know when to give a little to gain a lot more."

"I see." Aldora sighed and leaned her forehead into his arm, exhausted. She found comfort in the flex of his muscles. "You've gained little with the way you are, everything else you've taken."

His fingers tugged at the ends of her hair. "There is nothing easy about living in the labyrinth. I do what I must."

She nuzzled, seeking comfort. "I'm learning."

"You are. What hell entered your mind when you decided to claw your wrist open?"

"You," she said, lifting her head to face him.

"The thought of me made you want to kill yourself?" His voice darkened.

"The thought of you made me do what I had to, to try and escape."

"Death is not an escape, female. Not here in this place. I've told you once before that there is no escape, and if you had died, I would have brought you back to this place screaming."

Aldora sat back, her energy waning. "I wasn't trying to die. I had no idea whether Alepos and his men had killed you or not, and I did not dare pry further in case they hadn't. There was little I could do but try to seduce them, or create more chaos. Chaos seems to follow me wherever I go." She shook her head. "I couldn't..." She shuddered thinking of the centaur's massive cocks. "I couldn't let them touch me, and then I remembered my blood. I only hoped for the best so I had a better chance at running."

He grunted, the tension expelling from his frame. "You can't outrun me, let alone a stud who wants to breed you."

Her stomach clenched. "I'm always willing to try."

Vedikus eyed her, and she knotted her fingers in her lap.

"I won't run from you," she amended.

"I would catch you. And it would hurt."

"I know."

She could feel his eyes trailing over her grubby clothes and dirty skin. The heat of his stare reminded her of their time together, how he'd cared for her wounds, and how he'd attempted to conquer her body. She tried to ignore it, the prickle of unease, the quick stab of want, the hollow, relentless ache, but whenever her life wasn't in immediate danger, those sensations came flooding back.

Everything about it was unsettling, more so that neither one of them was in any shape to ease the lust that lingered and bloomed, oftentimes bursting between them. *Lust.* She could almost taste it on her lips. It was consuming when it exploded. She moved to sit on her legs, pressing the heel of her boot hard against her sex.

Vedikus continued to watch her, reading her, and she

skirted her gaze away to the shadows. *If I can pretend he's not here, I can pretend the tension is an illusion.* She wanted to laugh at her absurdity.

"Human," he said, his voice grave.

"Are we safe?" she asked, trying not to drown.

"Female," Vedikus warned lower, deeper, wrong. His presence grew to encompass her space.

"No."

He grabbed her, dragging her toward him, grasping what was left of her tunic. His arms came around her, caging her against his body. She pushed away from him.

"Your wounds," she gasped, feeling the stab of his cock against her side. "They'll open!"

Vedikus grabbed her hair and forced her head back, making her mouth part and her legs kick out. Her pulse hammered. He forced her to look at him.

"Answer me this, Aldora, and I may let you go." She dug her nails into his chest. The warmth had returned to his body. "Why did you risk your life to escape? The centaurs would have protected and guarded you."

She licked her lip. "I told you already."

His gaze narrowed darkly. "You told me you were going to run." He paused. "Not what you would have done afterward."

Her palms fell flat on his chest, and her throat constricted. She wanted to keep her secrets inside, hidden away from being released into the world. Her motivations had changed so abruptly she had yet to catch up. Aldora wondered when she had come to accept her life here on the other side of the wall.

He's inside me. I swallowed his name. Vedikus's presence

had filled every hole and hidden place she had left, Following him to Prayer hadn't been about survival, it had been about curing her illness, about extending her life. And for what? To expunge the mist from her body so she wouldn't lose herself to mindlessness?

To spend more time with the beast?

A small part of her hoped that by curing it, she'd be free of him. That he was part of the curse and just needed to be banished. Another, stronger part of her focused on that tendril of hope despite the lie beneath.

He warned me from the beginning. There's no escape.

No cure for exorcising him.

"I would have—" The words that came out were heavy. "I would have looked for you."

"Why?"

"To know if you were dead."

"And would you have finished me off if I were not?"

"No," she answered. His lips twitched, bringing her attention to his mouth.

Vedikus drew her closer until she lost sight of it and his breath drifted through her own parted lips. An almost kiss. "Why?"

"Because I cared! I care."

His mouth twisted up into a smile. The first wisp of steam drifted up over his face to caress his blunt features. She licked her lower lip, wishing she could taste the salt of his sweat against them.

"I wanted to be with you," she said gently.

Vedikus pulled her away, and with strength she thought he no longer possessed, moved her over him until she straddled his hips, never releasing her hair. There was a look of triumph on his face, and it made her confession all that much harder. Aldora lifted off him only to be jostled back into position. A blush stung her cheeks as his shaft pressed and moved against her.

His other hand lingered on her lower back, slipping under her tunic to settle over her skin. She was afraid to place her own on his body, unable to see the extent of his wounds under the bandages, and settled to touch only where he was exposed.

"I am a warrior. Pain is nothing," he said as if he read her mind. "Mount me." Vedikus pushed his hips up.

"No." Aldora tried to look over her shoulder at the shadowy entrance, but he kept her anchored his way.

"You've already admitted you have nothing else to live for, female. Don't stop yourself now."

"I never admitted such a thing," she snapped. "You think too highly of yourself. I would never—" His hand wrenched her hair back and a gasp escaped her lips. His mouth crashed onto hers, claiming the shallow space between.

She jerked under the pressure and parted her lips further, succumbing to his unspoken demand. Like everything about him, the kiss was rough and greedy, taking every intimate space she had left and claimed it for his own. His overly large hands roamed her body, warming her through her ruined, wet clothes. She melted into him, seeking his heat, and a strange sense of comfort overcame her.

She found it hard to breathe, hard to find her bearings with his focus solely on her. It happened every time Vedikus touched her with intention, with crude, unsolicited want that he laid bare before her. She was forced to acknowledge it, being captured at his side whether it was by rope, by his grip, or his will, she was always within the reach of his desire.

I can remember his smell. Vedikus cupped the back of her head and reared over her, bending her back and feasting on her mouth. *I can't taste him.* Aldora imagined it was brimstone and oil, filled with the hottest spices from south of the capital. *The only thing that belongs to his heat.*

She kissed him back at last and took his phallic tongue with her teeth, trapping it in the way she felt trapped, drawing a low hum from his throat. It shot through her and built the hollow ache between her legs. The stretch and burn from his abrupt taking hours prior teased her core, waking it back up despite the horror, drenching her undergarments with her essence.

His cock stabbing its way through her pants was her only relief. Her sex constricted, dying for his prick to penetrate her deep and hard. She undulated what she could of her hips, rubbing her swollen, needy self all over him.

His groping hands moved up her chest, skimming over her nipples before he gripped the collar of her tunic. She released his mouth when his violent fingers shredded her shirt down the middle, not even leaving her thin underwear to cover her chest.

Vedikus cupped her breasts and squeezed, rubbing the pads of his thumbs across her beaded nipples in torturous circles. Aldora rocked her hips helplessly.

"Females of my kind do not have full, rounded tits," he said, his dark gazed focused upon them. "There's nothing soft about them like these."

"There's nothing soft about you," she whimpered when he pinched her.

"You'll be my soft."

He tugged at her nipples and rubbed them in quick circles, his head bowed, watching them. She grasped his wrists to keep her seated on his bulge. Aldora squirmed as the pressure became uncomfortable, and the pawing became obsessive, demanding, and raw. She pulled back, but was stilled by his growl. Not even the young men she had slept with in Thetras acted so consumed with her body, so intent on possessing it. A sliver of fear coursed through her.

Vedikus isn't human.

His eyes met hers with a demonic smile. His horns glinted green from the low light. "I will not want to share your mother's milk with our offspring."

She pursed her lips but was attacked again by his. They beat her back and sucked on her own and she winced from the pain. Vedikus drew back to soften the blow, licking the hurt away. Aldora squeezed his wrists.

His mouth drew away from hers, trailing down her neck to flick his tongue over the tips of her nipples. His tongue was larger, rougher, with a slight sandpaper effect to accompany its wetness, and the abraded feel of it left her hungering for more, for it to continue its trail past her breasts. He tongued her nipples, easing the soreness from his fingers. Aldora arched into his mouth. He sucked and pulled, sending her body dancing upward seeking relief.

She grabbed his horns and tensed for the onslaught. His hand grasped the front of her pants and pulled, drawing her into him until she heard the snap of the seams rip and the release of the cloth. She gasped and pushed back. "My only clothes," she murmured, finding it hard to exhale.

"You'll wear me, female," he grunted, tearing off what was left of her clothing and bringing it to his face. He buried his nose in it. Aldora let go of him and covered her breasts, unsure of her nudity.

She watched as his gaze met hers over her ruined coverings. "We can't stay here forever."

Vedikus didn't answer as he breathed in the scent of her clothes, making her nervous. His muscles strained, hardening before her eyes. His bulge shifted where she sat on it, swelling as his body grew. The change wasn't subtle, it was the same as when he fought, and each second that it continued, it built. Her chest tightened and her brow furrowed. She shifted away slightly, feeling the need to distance herself from him, but the moment she moved, he dropped her clothes and pressed her back into the stone floor.

Her world spun as she was rolled over, pawed at, and she was shocked by how much smaller she was to him. His hands raised her hips off the ground, and Aldora flattened her palms out in front of her, bracing herself.

She felt the sting of his cock press heavily at her opening where it slipped across her exposed sex. It was wet, wetter than just her own essence leaking out of her, and she stiffened wondering what it was.

"Wait!" she cried, but it came out too late. She released a shriek that ended on a long, pained moan. He slammed into her, sending her body forward. Everything went black as she was stretched forcibly, brutally, harder than any time before.

He grabbed her hair and raised her cheek from the floor. "If you do not mount me, I will mount you, female. Do not presume that I will beg," he snarled, pounding her hips into the ground.

She didn't get a chance to adjust to him, didn't have a moment to ease into his possession as dirt coated her lips. She had never had a chance. From their first meeting to being thrown over the wall, there had never been any ease of transition.

She came out stronger for it in the end.

Aldora relaxed as much as she could and accepted his ferocity, giving herself over to it and letting it fill her up. Her nails raked across the stone floor, catching a small trail of dust beneath their beds. Her lips kissed the ground as his legs hit the back of hers. They were velvet and slightly rough, the hair that thickened across them at once soft and coarse. Like fur.

She lifted her front off the stone that abraded her skin and onto her forearms, shuddering as she was rammed forward and then yanked back, each happening in rapid succession but with changing momentum. His large, torn hands grasped her waist and kept her in place.

"Please," she gasped, finding strands of her tangled hair plastered to her face, distorting the room. Vedikus squeezed her middle and she dipped her head. His bull's cock stretched her sex and filled her to the brink, forcing her to take more. She cried out.

Her core tightened, and her back was blasted with a gust of hot air. Aldora pressed her forehead into the floor and it scrapped for several thrusts before she picked herself up again and reached between her thighs.

The grunts coming from behind built, arching her lower half up and down quickly off the floor. There were jolts of pain but they lessened with each pump of his hips. Aldora found the strength to press back and meet his next thrust, finding his cock growing increasingly slippery. That slick spread to dribble down her legs and between their rocking hips, speeding up their movements.

Her knees knocked the floor.

Aldora strummed her clit and dared to look over her shoulder, through the strands of her hair.

Vedikus reared up, his head bowed, his gleaming green-lit horns aimed at her head. He leered at where their bodies met, staring at where his cock stabbed her. Heat pooled her sex. *I'm finally filled with him.* She dug her nails into the ground and tried to hold herself up. Vedikus's mouth lowered into a sneer just as she was shunted forward.

A roar echoed off the walls.

Aldora dropped to the ground and she felt the heavy weight of his body shell her own, ramming in quick, short thrusts. More grunts were strangled out, and a moan left her lips as Vedikus filled her with seed. It gushed from his cock, out of her sex, and pooled down her thighs.

She thought she could smell it, was almost able to convince herself that she had. It was salty and raw.

Time passed and his shallow ramming continued, his breaths fanned the back of her head. She squirmed, uncomfortable beneath him as she was forced to take even more of his spurts. Aldora shivered and tapped at her clit, moving weakly in the small space she had and found her own bliss. She found it again as his bull's head rubbed endlessly against a pleasurable spot inside her, milking more contractions from her sex. What had started out as a frenzy turned into an obsessive need to take pleasure from each other without giving any back.

She danced under him, her body writhing, seeking more.

"Vedikus…" It was a long-winded, charged moan between spasms. "W-what's happening?"

A thick arm snaked between her and the floor, picking her up and moving her until she straddled his lap. She slid down his length, his prick spreading her wider. Aldora winced. Her palms moved up his arms, over his thick neck to cup his face. The soles of her feet touched the hard plates of his hooves and she wiggled her toes against the strangeness of him.

"You're mating a minotaur." His voice was gruff. He jostled her and her insides quivered. Another spurt shot from his cock and she braced for the pressure. It covered their privates, their legs, even the stone floor where her knees now glided across. "I could not wait any longer for my prize."

"No," she gasped as his hands gripped her and moved her on him. Aldora buried her face into the crook of his neck and relinquished all control. She chased her bliss as he used her.

Vedikus quickened his fucking, pistoning up while slamming her back down.

"Vedikus," she wailed, every fiber of her body shaking.

NAOMI LUCAS

It was too raw, too wet. Aldora wrapped her fingers around
his bull horns and held on.

When it became too much, he rose up, taking her lower
half with him. Her upper back hit the cold stone with
force. Her legs fell to the sides, spread eagle as he
hammered brutally into her, his meaty legs trapping her in
position.

Vedikus roared again over her face, coming like a beast
in heat, spearing her body in half.

Aldora sank to the floor, spent, used, and warmed to
her darkening soul. Steam filled the air between them,
rising from his nose and mouth as he held her bruisingly,
and with each second that passed, with each twitch of his
cock, his lust diminished into spent relief. She licked the
tears from her lips. He removed his hands from her waist,
making her shudder when his bulge pulled out.

He peered down at her sharply, nostrils flaring, eyes
alight with arrogance. Conquest. Dark intent. She could do
nothing but catch her breath and gaze up at him.

"You look best when being bred, Aldora."

She didn't think she had it in her to blush again, but
felt one on her cheeks all the same. Many things had
changed in the past span of days, but this was one change
she was at peace with. The one thing that gave her
power. Vedikus had proven his intent with her safety and
his need for her, and she knew she had proven her
loyalty.

"Have I been?" she asked softly.

"When a bull ruts for pleasure, his seed does not need
to be released to find it, but when we rut for real, it is a
messy affair." He cupped her aching sex making her hips

jerk, and his hand came away with clear, thick cum. "I was determined to have you."

"You do not know yet then?" If she had been bred. They looked at his hand. He dipped it into the water and cleaned it with the displaced towel, then he wiped them both down. The water was cool against her skin.

"My body has been priming since I first heard your voice. Days of torment plagued me to lay my claim."

She remembered his persistent erection. It comforted her knowing she had not been sacrificed to the maze as a virgin. She would not have known what was entailed otherwise.

"Was it because I was a human?".

"It was your voice."

"My voice?" she inquired further.

"It was… I needed more of it."

Aldora licked her lips. "I found yours pleasing as well," she admitted weakly. "I still do." It was the first thing of his that had filled her, had made her feel something more than fear in this place.

Vedikus dropped the cloth and moved to the fire pit. He picked up the blackened logs within and breathed upon them. She curled her arm under her head and watched as golden light cast out the eerie green of the room. The walls lit up in shades of silver-hued yellow and licks of copper, and she sighed, at once comforted by the light but disquieted, seeing Alepos's body again in her head.

Aldora turned away and faced the archway that led deeper into the temple. Something flitted deep inside and she lifted up, squinting into the darkness.

She's watching. Her mouth parted to call out right when

a heavy arm draped over her side, and a broad chest pressed into her back. Vedikus pulled her against him with a weary sigh. "You have pleased me this night, human. I will remember."

Her eyes closed briefly as she let his words envelop her. *Pleased.* She tested out her muscles and found them languid where they had been tense and that a contented, wary exhaustion had replaced her need to fight. Aldora pressed the back of her hand to her lips and settled in. Vedikus's chest warmed her back.

"You've pleased me too," she whispered as they rested.

Chapter Seventeen

She could not sleep, her gaze never leaving the shadows. Vedikus had long since fallen into slumber beside her. She waited for the hag to approach; Aldora knew she was there, and it was only a matter of time.

When the girl finally revealed herself, Aldora was ready, taking a moment to slip out from under her minotaur's weight. She hesitated, waiting to see if she had awoken him, but his arm relaxed to the floor, and his dreams remained undisturbed.

The hag—with the face of a young girl—handed her an old, frayed, white shift which Aldora donned silently, listening to the popping snap of the dying fire.

Aldora followed the young woman from the room and deeper into the stone passageways. The tunnels were similar to those she encountered within the barrier lands, but less overgrown, less wild, and were clearly part of an overall design. Despite outward appearances, it was a lived in structure that was taken care of. She trailed her fingers along the wall when the vines near it suddenly burst out toward her with thorns. She snatched her hand back, remembering their pain.

"They protect themselves." The girl looked back. "Like everything else here, they're a product of living in a cruel world."

Aldora tangled her fingers into the shift the girl had given her. "What's your name?"

"Hypathia. No? Nithers, then," the girl said with a sly grin. "Maybe my name is Alepos, Aldora, or Vedikus. What does it matter?"

What? Aldora's eyes widened. "How do you know?"

"I sensed your presence, and I knew your minotaur's intention to come here the moment you entered the wetlands. I don't just let anyone find this place. You can call me Calavia." The girl turned away and continued down the hall, only to duck into the shadows of another room. Aldora sped up to catch her. "Those who seek to raid or to hurt me or mine will never find this place."

The vines stopped at the entrance to accumulate into large masses around the doorway where the hag entered. Beyond was an altar. It was cluttered with candles of every length and size, and more than half were lit. The wax fell in thick streams down their stems to drip off the sides where it collected in a puddle on the floor. Calavia sat next to where it ended, like a slow-building wave of molasses.

Aldora wanted to rush to her side and pull her away despite the wax not moving. The sudden urge made Aldora pause, and she remained where she was, taking the girl in. Calavia's hair was as long as her own, but darker, with strands that seemed to absorb the light instead of reflecting it. It was unwashed and matted with visible mud caked it, making it appear heavy, and it fell in hardened clumps over her rags.

She's untrustworthy. And yet, Aldora's hands ticked at her sides to touch her.

"Are you human?" she asked, ducking under the archway, making sure not to touch the vines.

"Not like you. I can't repel the curse, but I was human, and still am in some small ways. I've never felt the sunlight. I believe to be human is to miss it but how can I miss something I've never felt?"

"I don't understand?" Aldora stopped a short distance away. "The sun has nothing to do with humanity."

"It does if that's where our people come from." Calavia idly caressed the stiff wax. "I can never cross the barrier even if I made it to the wall."

"Have you tried?" *Could she help me get back?* Aldora glanced at the shadowy exit behind her. Vedikus was asleep somewhere beyond, healing from the hurts he sustained on her behalf, drunk on her blood. *Filled with my blood as I'm filled with his seed.* She shifted on her feet, feeling the thick cum inside her, still leaking out from her core where he had filled it so entirely. Even though she had cleaned herself, more replaced what was taken away, reminding her she would never be free from him… or the life he had planned for her.

I could be with child…

She placed her hands on her belly. *I could be...*

"I have not." The hag looked at her sharply, scattering her excited thoughts. "I would not try even if I could. There is nothing on the other side that appeals to me."

"Not even safety?" Aldora shook her head. "Never mind. Anyone with magic in Savadon is considered deviant and evil…" she trailed off, considering. "There's nothing for you there."

Calavia smiled up at her. "Apparently not."

"But I'm…at a loss. You look human, you have magic, and Vedikus knows about you. How have you survived in such a horrid place alone? I've seen more…things die trying to capture me than I can name, even chasing me across the terrain." She thought about the centaurs, of Alepos's burning horseflesh.

The hag broke off a piece of wax and began to move it between her hands. It changed shape, taking on the malleability of putty but did not drip between the girl's fingers. Eventually, it took on the shape of a doll that resembled the hag, down to the details of the wrinkles of Calavia's rags.

"Creatures such as me have nothing to offer but their ability to manipulate. I was born here in this very bog, long ago, back when the labyrinth was smaller, and the walls bordered the mountains. Prayer was a bordertown that protected the lands of humans from what was within. The day I was conceived was the day this place succumbed. Everyone who survived, including my mother, became a thrall except for me. It happens that way sometimes." Calavia placed the doll back onto the mountain of wax where it lay within its shape, undisturbed. "Bad things always have a bad start. My mother is still alive, wandering through what is left if you'd like to see her."

Aldora shook her head and wiped her palms against the folds of her shift, remembering why she was there to begin with. "The curse made them that way," she stated more than questioned.

"Yes."

"Vedikus brought me here because you could cure it."

"I can."

"Will you cure me?"

Calavia reached into her shirt and plucked out a small vial-shaped cylinder made from the same wax she sat next to. Like the rest, it was a pale, pasty white with a tinge of yellow, but smoothed to a gleam even beyond that of the detailed doll. "Everything comes at a price."

Aldora would pay it. "What is yours?" She could already feel other changes happening within her body beside her abrupt loss of smell and taste. Her hands had yet to leave her belly, and she clenched them together.

"A life."

She immediately thought of the possibility of the child that could be in her womb, and the fear she hadn't felt earlier crashed into her. "I don't have a life to give," she breathed, dropping her hands.

"I think you do." Calavia pointedly looked at Aldora's stomach.

Aldora stiffened but didn't take a step back. "I don't. I can't give you that, please ask for something else," she said, leaving the words unspoken between them. Did she want to know if she carried? Part of her screamed to know while the other part flooded her with panic.

The hag laughed softly and placed the makeshift vial down next to the doll. "Is that too steep for you, Aldora?"

"Yes."

"I would ask for the life of your unborn child."

She stilled. "So I'm pregnant?" she rushed out.

Calavia dipped her head. "I don't know."

"Then how can I give you something I don't have?"

"You own your own life, do you not?"

Vedikus owns my life. The words sat on the tip of her tongue. *Vedikus has taken everything there was left of me.* "I don't." An odd sense of relief came upon her when she admitted it. A burden lifted. Vedikus owned her and she accepted it, even felt safer, freer, now that the choice was out of her hands.

"You own the minotaur," Calavia said, breaking her thoughts once again.

A laugh escaped her lips before she could stop it. "I don't have it in me to make a claim such as that."

"You have his seed still running down your legs. Don't deny it. I can smell it over the soil, but how would you know that? Minotaur semen is potent and you've lost your sense of smell."

"You seem to know a lot."

"More than you." Calavia smiled eerily. "You have exactly what I want."

Something ran down her inner thigh and she knew what the girl wanted. There were only so many ways to bring life into this world and the minotaur's seed was one of them. The hag wasn't bargaining for her unborn child, but for the potential of giving old semen another chance. Was it hers to give?

"What would you do with it?" Aldora had to know before handing it over. The thought of Calavia swelling with Vedikus's child made her bristle. *I've earned my place.* Her hand went back to her stomach. She'd grown used to being by his side, within his presence, even in the harrowing, short time they had been together. If she was damned to this place, and even given what she'd seen, there was no place she would rather be. Safe. Protected. And well away from the monsters that sought more than a piece of her soul.

Calavia shuffled on her knees. "We all need things to survive in this place. Seed such as his will help me protect this land and myself."

"You won't use it to bring life into this place?" She was already thinking of ways to kill Calavia depending on her answer.

The girl smiled again, brighter than before. "I only seek to protect myself and my thralls, human. You're welcome to stay here and become one of them if you so choose. My price is low, considering, and if you have learned anything about the mist, prices are often more than any willing being is wanting to pay. Do you want to see your home again?"

"I…" do. But the word went unspoken. Aldora looked down at her hands, the broken nails on her fingers, the cuts healing on her skin. "I'm not sure." When she thought of home, she thought of apples, not her family or her mother's farm, and especially not Thetras, not anymore. Apples: red and juicy and tangible, fresh and sweet with juices making her hands sticky. Like Vedikus's seed drying on her inner thighs. "I'm not sure."

"You'll never see it if you become nothing."

Aldora's gaze snapped back to Calavia, pulling out another wax vial from her rags. "Neither one of us want to become nothing."

"No," she agreed, twitching. "And there is nothing else you want?"

"Not from you."

"Not even my blood?"

"I have plenty. You're not the first human brought to me, nor will you be the last." Calavia crawled to sit directly before Aldora's legs, looking up at her with excited eyes, the vial clutched to her chest.

Aldora swallowed, looking down at the girl, anxious but excited, wanting to reflect the same look back at the hag. Part of her wanted to turn on her heel and wake up Vedikus so he could take the decision from her hands. It made her feel like a coward, knowing she wanted to crawl to him like Calavia had crawled to her. She wanted his hand in her hair as he looked down at her. There were no apples in the picture, just him and her, and if anything was between her hands or her thighs, it was him.

Vedikus would not leave here without curing me. Calavia reached out and played with the folds of Aldora's shift.

Aldora looked back at the exit.

A hand tugged her skirt. "This is a transaction between women. My price will not change even if you brought him here."

"He could kill you," Aldora muttered.

A laugh. "He could try, but are you really selfish enough to deny all the beings that will come after you for help?"

There had been another sacrifice after hers. "No," she said. Whoever it was could end up here.

"Then let this be over."

Calavia lifted and cinched up the excess cloth fluttering

around Aldora's legs. She stared at the girl and watched quietly as her bare legs were revealed. The vial was uncapped and the waxen rim ran up her leg, catching some of what continued to trickle out of her. It disappeared within Calavia's shirt a moment later.

Aldora walked back to the pool room with the cure firmly in her hand, uncertain about what she had just done.

Chapter Eighteen

"Wake up."

Vedikus's eyes snapped open and a solemn, second-hand light flooded his vision. It had the likings of a berserk but with a calmness around the intent. Intently relaxed instead of intently violent. He had not awakened like this since the days of his youth, since his bedding was a nest of leathers, and his many brothers slept at his side. He would never be the first one awake; his mother and his elder brother were always up before him.

Not much had changed. As an adult minotaur, he was not the first one to rise, again.

Aldora kneeled at his side with just the tips of her fingers brushing his arm.

"You may touch more of me if you wish," he rumbled, searching her face and finding it exhausted where his would most likely appear well-rested. Her fingertips left his skin and he missed her touch immediately. He could become enthralled with it, he knew, touches that were meant for pleasure instead of pain. It would weaken him, and yet, he allowed himself to miss it. Vedikus reached up to swipe her hair over her shoulder. "You did not sleep."

She was beautiful. And despite the hardship that the labyrinth had placed on her, his female had grown more beautiful to him since he caught her that first night. He had not lied when he said that she was all that would be soft about him. Acknowledging his weakness had changed him. Vedikus flicked his tail. He was stronger for it.

We both are.

"I didn't want to risk dreaming." Her face fell and he tugged a rebellious strand of her hair. It was another soft touch against him, a silken touch this time. *I will craft her a comb made from the bones of our enemies.* "If I dreamt something sweet, then I would never want to wake up, but if I had a nightmare…"

"I'm sorry," he said abruptly. Aldora's eyes shot to his, widening with shock. The word was unusual on his tongue, but it did not worry him. If he could wake like this—refreshed—and with her each morning, it was a small price to pay. "I hurt you."

"I may have…" She glanced away for a brief moment. "I've hurt you more." Aldora shifted and peeled back the old bandages across his middle. He felt nothing but the pressure of the old material lift from his flesh. The stabs to his gut had healed over, and the outer edges were crusted over with old blood. Vedikus dropped his hand into the pool on the other side of him and wiped it clean.

"And have healed my pains many times over. I have not risen to greet the day with jubilation in longer than I can remember. Your blood is sweet and remains in me."

"It doesn't hurt? I can't believe how fast you've recovered. Are you sure it's not this place and the magic that is here?"

"Any hurts would be welcomed. It means I have paid for my life this day, but no, I do not hurt, not in the way you suggest, female, but I'm not fully recovered." He sat up. His gaze dropped from her face to the new clothes she wore. A shift that was white, stained but clean—at least as clean as any cotton could be here. "The hag of Prayer has given you a boon."

Aldora flinched. "She has given us more."

His gaze narrowed as she turned away and pulled a plate forth. On it lay boiled roots and strips of pink meat that he could not place, but it was the pale cylinder of wax beside it. He picked it up to find the top was a cork made of the same material. Something sloshed around inside. *Could it be?*

Vedikus looked back at Aldora. "Eat," he demanded and returned his attention back to the vial.

She sighed and the sound of her chewing slowly filled the quiet space.

He gingerly removed the cap, murmuring a rite against whatever lay within for protection, and slowly pulled it off. The stench of it filled the air immediately. The cove was the first scent that hit him but it wasn't the one he was looking for. There was wight root and salt, bone powder and blisterwood smoke, but it was the magic laced into it he wanted. To him, magic had a smell, or a touch that made tangible things intangible. It was ever changing, but strong. He felt Aldora's gaze on him.

Vedikus lowered the vial. "It is safe. How did you get it?"

She stopped chewing and swallowed. "She gave it to me after we spoke."

"When did you speak?" His eyes narrowed.

"Last night when you were resting. I couldn't sleep, not after everything that had happened, and I knew she was there." Aldora pointed to the passage. "When she came, she offered me the dress and asked me to follow her. I knew what had to be done."

Anger bloomed. "You did not think to wake me?"

"No. I did not," she said with such assurance it took him aback. Defiance was not something he had come to know from her.

"Why?"

"Because I knew she would not hurt me—us—after we had entered her space. It was a woman's conversation that needed to happen, and I—" she paused, "we needed to speak alone."

Many things came to his skull about what the hag would have wanted. What she could have offered Aldora... He had slept well last night, too well, and he did not think it was entirely to do with his and Aldora's rutting, her blood fueling his veins, or the healing of his wounds. Vedikus checked for his battle axes and found them by the burned-out fire where he had set them the night before.

"What did she offer you?" he asked, anger simmering amongst his wariness. *A way home? A way to be rid of me?* He looked hard at the half-eaten food. *No.* Aldora could not kill him, even if she poisoned him with witch spit, even if she leaned over him in the throes of sleep to slit his throat.

She did not have the strength to pierce through his layers of skin and muscle and do any real damage.

Vedikus took quick stock of his injuries and found them all well and on their way to being healed. There were no new marks felt or seen on his flesh.

Aldora pursed her lips. *She's hiding something.* "Only the vial and its contents, that and the conveniences of dress and this food. She offered me nothing else."

He did not believe her. "And you did not ask for a way home?"

Aldora startled and looked away. He followed her gaze to her clenched hands. "I thought about it, but did not."

"Why?"

"I realized there is nothing for me there now. Like there is nothing for a woman such as the hag, who could enter Savadon if she so chose. I would never be accepted back."

That gave him pause. He knew very little of the ways of humans beyond the barrier but knew they ruled in large numbers over vast lands. "You could not go elsewhere?"

"I could, but they say those that make it back from the mists come back marked. They're shunned and often removed out of sight, to be forgotten. They're never spoken of or seen again. I have not met one, but I have heard the stories." She chuckled suddenly, softly, briefly. "So many stories."

"And you believe this even after all you know has been untrue?" His curiosity was piqued. Vedikus knew some humans made it back, if only because the centaurs used such means as leverage. *But a mark?* He reached for Aldora and pulled her close, momentarily forgetting his suspicion, and pulled up her shift. The female shivered in his embrace as he trailed his fingers over her skin, making his own tense to react.

He tempered his sudden need to flip her over and bury his cock deep when she spoke. "I don't know what I believe, but I did not ask Calavia to go back. We only spoke as women, as women often do, and she gave me the cure."

Vedikus pressed his outspread hands over her smooth back, remembering how her pale spine moved as he mounted her hours earlier. *Like silken thread.* And lowered his mouth to her ear. "I know you're lying." She stiffened further, but all he did was hold her naked body against his. "Do not deny it or find my wrath. I rode you hard, I can ride you harder still, Aldora." Her shallow breaths warmed his chest. His bulge stirred to lengthen and rest upon his thigh. New seed brewed deep in his loins. "Tell me," he warned, raising her chin.

Her clothing was still bunched up between them and he lowered it to cover her, wanting to stop her shaking. He found he did not like her discomforted, even by his own hand. Vedikus restrained more than his body's need for her at that moment. *If she is not cold, she's afraid.* His threats against her were shallow at best, but it reminded him of the hundreds of times his sire had handled his mother.

There had always been firm, simmering heat between them, and when it boiled over, curses filled the stable of their home. His parent's fights were as heated and as deep as their love for each other.

Vedikus stiffened, dropping his hand back down to Aldora's back. He found he wanted to touch more of her, and if he couldn't, he wanted to hold her impossibly tight against him. She was safe in his embrace, and the idea that she had left his side, even when she had the freedom to do so, made him nervous.

The centaurs almost took her from me.

Never again.

If he had to tie her up, tie her to him for the rest of their lives, he was willing to do that if it resulted in giving him peace of mind.

"The hag asked for one thing…" she murmured, her head resting under his chin.

Her body? Her blood? Locks of her hair? He would not have her barter her own being after all that she had already lost. His anger flared again. "What?" *Everything she owns belongs to me. How dare she assume otherwise...*

"Protection for her and her thralls."

Vedikus wrapped his mind around her words. "And how do you expect to give her something like that? You may be able to save yourself, but another? And one who is not me or part of our clan? That request is void upon asking it." His confusion grew. Whether it was a lich, a witch, warlock, or hag bargaining their services, one thing was always the same. They never gave their services unless they had received their end of the deal.

"She will not use it for anything but strengthening her defense of Prayer."

"She will not use what?" He pushed Aldora back and searched her face. It was less sun-kissed than before. The mist's pallor had begun to take the color from her skin. She gripped his forearms and her nails bit into him. "Use what?' he asked again, wracking his skull for any possibilities.

"Your seed."

Vedikus peeled his hands from her and shook her off. "You gave her my…" He could not finish the words, dropping his gaze to the crux of her thighs.

"It was the only thing she wanted. Please." Aldora wrung her hands. "She would accept nothing else, and I tried. I offered her all that I could, but she knew it was still fresh between my legs. I thought she meant to bargain for our first child! Anything asked was better than that, anything. I would never make a child pay for the sins of another."

He barely heard her words. His eyes stared where the cloth of her shift was bunched up in her lap.

Trickery.

"Vedikus…"

"Do not!" he snapped. "Do not say my name in such a way, female. And what may I ask, did she want with my lifeforce?" His muscles tensed and he ached to break something. He imagined the worst possible outcome. Vedikus saw Aldora's belly grow with his offspring. It all flashed through his skull in quick succession.

"She said it was for protection."

"And did you think to ask how it would protect?"

"Yes! Listen to me, please—"

"—would you have told me this if I hadn't asked?"

Aldora lowered her head.

His anger grew.

"She would have nothing else," she continued.

Lies! And yet he knew it was the truth the moment it

left her lips. Vedikus reached for his axes, sending Aldora staggering to the ground on her backside, her legs tangling in thin material. He wanted to rip it clean off her and force her nudity in his presence.

"Please," she gasped. "She swore it was for nothing else, and nothing else would satisfy her. What would you have had me do?"

"I would have had you sleeping by my side while I dealt with the bitch!" he roared, releasing steam hot enough to sear into the air. "She'll die this daybreak." He rose to his hooved feet, stamping one down to crack the stone beneath. Aldora looked up at him wide-eyed with fear. Vedikus went for the exit.

"She's gone," she rushed to say, and he felt a tug on the back of his leathers. Aldora stopped him, and he turned, sneering.

"Where?"

She shook her head and he was momentarily transfixed by the way her hair moved in the subtle light. "It was either your seed or my life," she pleaded. "Your seed or nothing else."

"The hag dies," he hissed, pressing his hand against her chest and pushing her back. Aldora refused to let go and he rounded to fully face her.

"After everything I've been through you will listen to me!" she yelled, startling him. "What is worth more to you? My life, which you so desperately saved at every opportunity, or control and authority? Did you think we would be handed what we needed with nothing on our bodies but bloodied rags and wounds? She could have asked for worse, could have asked for so much more, but she did not. I've sacrificed enough and was willing to sacrifice more. Now you know how it feels to lose something you did not want to lose." She released him and returned to the ashen fire pit, taking a plate of food.

Vedikus stared after her for a time, feeling his blood pumping through his veins, his rage darkening to simmer into something else. He wanted to feel bones snap between his fingers, to hear the struggle of his enemies falling before him. His palms dampened with sweat as other sensations poured through him, like how he wanted to feel Aldora back in his arms, to struggle within his grasp, but with a look of pleasure on her face instead of pain.

She faced away from him and would not turn back to meet his eyes. He detested that he did not know what happened between her and the hag, but he knew Aldora was right. The hag was gone. He could no longer sense her presence among all the dead that inhabited Prayer. Looking for her now would just be a wasted effort and time they could spend elsewhere.

Light began to stream in powdery, grey wisps through the cracks in the ceiling and he knew they could no longer linger. Vedikus looked down at the vial still resting in his hand. The edges of the wax slipped with the first hints of melting from his body heat.

Was his seed, old seed given to her, worth more than her life?

His rage tempered in the silence as Aldora finished up the meal, not leaving a single morsel behind.

"I do not relish not knowing what the hag could use it for," he said, finding a hard-earned calmness return to his voice. The steam roiling in his lungs dispersed to be absorbed back into his body. He turned back toward the shadowy passageway. "We will leave for my lands when you are done. By nightfall we will be in the mountains."

"I trust her," Aldora's voice trailed after him, but he did not turn back.

And I trust you.

Chapter Nineteen

Aldora stood on the final broken step of the temple before the rest disappeared into the grasses and muck of the bog. She could already feel her boots sink into the mud and hated every second of it. She would hate it more when it was real. There was little left on her person but for some provisions she had pilfered from Calavia.

Stolen. The plants they plucked from within lay in hastily crafted knotted bags at her waist, made from her ruined cambric. The excess cloth she had left as payment, cleaned and folded.

She watched Vedikus return, stalking his way out of the mist. Anger had molded his features since that morning and she knew she had lost his trust. She did not want to lie to him nor evade the truth, but she was out of her element. If there had been another way, she would have taken it. It infuriated her that he was angry.

Aldora sighed, feeling defeated and nervous.

"Did you find her?" she asked as he approached, his hooves splashing water and his short tail swinging.

"She is gone."

"And the encampment? Were there any survivors? Have any of them made it to Prayer?" None had shown up after them to disturb them during the night. It had always been a possibility, but she was uncertain whether the hag would allow it or not.

The fact that she still had all her blood and new clothes —although they would not hold up long—had given her a sense of dependence on the place. She did not want to depend upon it. Her eyes moved back and forth over the faded landscape.

"Three have survived and are in the process of burning out the rest of their camp. If they do not head back to the shore, they will come here and seek vengeance."

"Let us leave now." She no longer felt safe staying in one place too long, even if that place had food and shelter.

He rounded on her, eyes glinting with agitation. "Are you so quick to flee, Aldora? You have received a gift from our host, have you not? From a host who never gifts freely. I would think you would want to stay here and settle."

She did not like him voicing her innermost thoughts. "I'm not fleeing," she said. "But I'm not willing to stay here either. It's too quiet…" The stillness unnerved her, and the flits of movement shrouded in white frightened her. The last thing she wanted was to remain in Prayer. "I choose to remain with you."

"You had no choice in that matter, now or ever," he snapped, eyes alight with sudden anger before vanishing again. She swallowed weakly. "It's the thralls." Vedikus had his hand over one of his axes. "They suck up the senses inside you then do the same to the land. This place is akin to an open wound so close to minotaur lands, but the hag and her minions have been here longer than my clan and will remain well after my bloodline is gone. Even in a land as dangerous as this, some things remain eternal." His gaze sharpened on her.

Her mouth went dry and she hugged her arms around herself. "I have not seen them."

The vial and its contents had not been given back to her to take. To see what she could become?

"Follow closely." Vedikus walked off the steps and back into the high grasses. "And say your goodbyes, we will not return. You will not want to."

Aldora rushed to his side, already knowing a goodbye was too much for this place.

The mist ballooned around her like a bubble in the early morning light to brighten up the strips of rotting wood cast about. She recalled it from the night before, but seeing the ghostly echoes of old life struck her in a way she hadn't expected. She'd seen ruins and stone walls, hedges, and broken monoliths, but the wood pallets were too close to home. *What would Vedikus's tribe be like?*

Ramshackle, decaying houses made from the same old wood appeared around her like monstrous sentinels in a quiet, grey field. Most no longer had doors, and those that did sat ajar and in pieces, hanging tenuously on rusted hinges. She peered inside the nearest one and saw broken crates and shadows, but nothing that would indicate the dwelling had an inhabitant.

Something moved inside, and she drew back.

Vedikus stopped a short ways away and waited. Aldora glanced from him and back to the shack, her legs tensing as she forced her unease deep inside. Groans and creaks, and bubbling pops sounded at her feet and from within. Shrouded by the mist, something approached, and she felt Vedikus's presence at her side.

His grounded aura assuaged her budding fear when a nearly naked elderly man stepped from the shack's shadows. He was followed shortly after by several others, all shrunken and pallid behind him, and all in varying states of dress. She sucked in a breath.

Dead white eyes met hers, emotionless, numb, hollowed of all that once made them human. One opened its mouth and moaned steadily, revealing grey, engorged gums where teeth should have been. Strips of long, nasty hair fell in stringy waves down their bodies, the same with their nails, which were spiraling away from their fingertips.

A screech and thump pricked her ears and she noticed that the old man was dragging a piece of wood. They all carried something. The two men that flanked the elderly one both possessed pitchforks.

Aldora took a step backward and into Vedikus's chest. His hand came up to rest on her shoulder.

"Why do they hold weapons?"

"The hag must have commanded them to do so. They do little of their own accord."

Calavia. Aldora glanced around, remember the hag's mother was supposedly among the creatures living in this place. "I want to leave."

More thralls made their way out of the fog and into her line of sight. Some with holes where eyes used to be,

220

some with mouths agape, while others who were less ghoulish gripped farm tools with preternatural ease.

Vedikus grunted but led her away. They walked slowly, steadily, through Prayer, leaving in the opposite direction from whence they came. She wanted to run—to escape this place as fast as possible—but was stopped by Vedikus's hold on her. It did not matter if sanctuary was found here. Aldora finally realized why she and Vedikus were the only outsiders. *Nobody comes here unless they have dire need.*

She desperately wanted to put as much distance between herself and this place as possible. Vedikus squeezed her arm to slow her.

"Do not move fast. They may decide you pose a threat."

She nodded and focused on putting one foot in front of the other. She steeled herself with looking forward and not around where several thralls were following them.

"Why are they following us?"

"For the same reason they are holding weapons."

They walked for some time in silence and she listened to the drudging footsteps of the things that trailed them. They were roars in her ears as more and more joined the first. She noticed Vedikus quietly, and very slowly, lift one of his axes from his side to rest in his hand when the splashes of distant, thundering steps sounded in the mist. It echoed back at them, growing louder with each passing second. Her eyes widened. Vedikus stilled. The thralls stumbled to a stop with them.

"Mist," Vedikus scowled, "we need to move." He walked ahead and tugged her forward. The others remained frozen, staring wordlessly as they passed.

"What is that?"

"Survivors," he hissed.

Aldora reached down and tugged the dagger from her boot and picked up her step, forgetting about the nearly lifeless bodies surrounding them. As they neared the outskirts of the settlement, dilapidated huts became rotting piles of wood, and their escorts dispersed. The noises grew more distant as they approached the lights leading out of Prayer, away from the centaurs who now sought their own sanctuary, and away from the eerie distress the old town wanted to drown her in.

Just as Aldora began to relax, she saw a lone figure that seemed to be waiting for the pair emerging from the mist, outside of the sphere of green light that marked the hag's domain. A middle-aged woman with hair that caught in the tall grasses stood before them. She was naked and pale to the point she nearly blended into the ashen fog.

But it was the bright red color of blood rushing down the woman's legs that took her aback.

Aldora shivered and squeezed her eyes shut, hoping the woman wouldn't be there when she reopened them, wishing she had never seen her in the first place.

Vedikus pressed her past the lone woman and she, too, faded into the landscape at their back.

They trekked for the rest of that morning and afternoon through the wetlands. Vedikus set a brutal pace and would not allow for long stops of rest. He kept his eyes upward and his ears to the world while keeping his hold on Aldora.

She staggered through the mud, and when the water was too deep, and the grasses too high, he lifted her into his arms and carried her through the worst.

She was lighter now, if subtly so, and he vowed to feed her a feast of his kills when she lay recovering in his nest of pelts. Vedikus pictured it, knowing it would be a reality soon. He was eager for a reprieve from the stresses of traveling with a human, one he had grown to care for deeply. He could still feel her pure blood traveling through his veins, bolstering his endurance. His brothers would help him in his endeavors and protect Aldora as if she were one of their own.

It did not sit well that he would have to rely on them, but he would suffer it if it meant he would have the added layers of safety for him and his own. It took a tribe to raise a calf. It would take all the Bathyr since it would be their first.

I look forward to it.

The vial sat heavily in a new pouch dangling from his leathers. A bubble of steam bloomed in his lungs. He would never know what happened between the hag and Aldora, but having the cure within his grasp was all that he cared about. The magic imbued in it left a trail that linked them with Prayer, and he knew that the hag and her legion would need to be dealt with at a later date. The settlement was too close to his mountain.

His seed—directly descended from the first bull—was strong, and the magic it created would be equally potent. After he and Aldora were settled, he would bring his brothers back and reclaim it.

If he was still angry, it was because she had left his side.

My mother disobeyed my sire at every turn. Vedikus looked down at Aldora resting with her head on his shoulder.

There is much to do. He would need to restock his personal stores to account for two for the coming seasons and prepare for his future offspring.

When his cloven feet hit dry land, the sun was already descending toward twilight. Vedikus squeezed Aldora gently.

"We have made it past the dregs, female. We will be within Bathyr lands by nightfall." He lowered her to the ground. She held onto him as she found her bearings.

"Will your clan accept me?"

"There is nothing to accept. You have mated with me and could even now be carrying a Bathyr in your womb. They will guard the clan's future with their lives." Vedikus led her away from the water. The strum of his heart lessened now that mud no longer sucked at his hooves.

"Are there... are there other humans?" Excitement colored her voice.

"No."

"Oh."

He tugged her hair. "You are the first and will not be the last. Astegur, my brother, is out in the wilds seeking out his own prizes and knowledge to bring back to the tribe. He may well return with a human if you seek to find comfort with your own kind."

"Astegur... Is he anything like you?" Aldora asked at his side, keeping pace. Vedikus had last seen his younger brother when they left the mountain together. Astegur was the weakest among them but rarely lost a battle when it came to wit. What his brother lacked in brutality, he compensated with craftiness.

"He likes a puzzle. Astegur was born third to my mother and is closest in age to me. We were reared together in my parent's stable and there is… competition between us. He will not like that I have found a mate before him, let alone a human one at that. No, we are not entirely alike but we are kin, and we were born with power, and so, overall yes, we are similar. The Bathyr all are."

"I have two younger sisters. We are alike but not, I understand."

"Then you understand loyalty."

"I would know what loyalty is regardless of my siblings. Loyalty is why I know I could never go back home because if I did, I would endanger them—put a target on their backs—and if that happened… I could never live with myself. I only hope they are okay and do not suffer for my actions."

His eyes sharpened on her. "I have not seen you cry for them."

She briefly met his gaze before turning away. "I did the first night."

Vedikus nodded. "And your loyalty, are you loyal to me?"

"I am."

He stopped and watched her as she took a couple steps forward before looking back to face him again. He had not expected her admission so easily and it helped soothe his displeasure. Aldora hugged herself against a chilly breeze at her back which sent her hair flying across her face. Vedikus closed the distance and burrowed his nose and mouth into the crook of her neck, breathing her in. She reached up and grabbed his horns as he licked her shoulder and neck. His body stirred, and he pulled back.

"You have my loyalty as well, human."

Aldora smiled softly and he puffed out his chest. They lingered in the moment for as long as possible, staring wordlessly at each other, and he tried to tell her everything and more with his eyes. *Home.* They would build one together. She took his hand and they continued with enough energy to renew their steps.

The ground changed as they began to ascend from the plains back to the rocky and uneven terrain of the highlands. There was no steep cliff this time, but a gradual climb, and they turned direction to follow the crags. He scanned the clearing for the signs of his clan.

Daylight still brightened the mist, but he could no longer see the tiny dot of the sun, and it wasn't until the faded orange haze of evening that they came upon the first marker. A gust of cold mountain air met them as they approached.

"A warning of the lands we are about to enter," he said. "Let me see your dagger." Vedikus waited as Aldora handed him the weapon and he pulled taut a small lock of her hair. "This will be a warning for all those who dare test us." He cut her hair and tied it to the post.

"To be afraid of me?"

"To know that this clan has braved the barrier lands and returned victorious, but yes, if it pleases you, all creatures in this place should fear your power as well."

She laughed softly, and he liked the sound. "I won't go

down without a fight. I knew that before in Thetras, but I know that more than ever, now."

"I have taught you bad habits," he teased back. A small smile curled on her lips and he found his own lowering toward them. The breeze blew her shift back, plastering it against her body, outlining what he enjoyed so much underneath.

"Will you teach me to fight? To wield my dagger and possibly even your axes to protect myself and to… protect us?"

Vedikus grasped her hand, finding her skin cool to the touch. "I will teach you more than that; you'll learn how to kill. You'll help make the Bathyr lands dangerous and our children will be feared throughout the world. They will need a mother who can meet them on the field."

Her smile grew. "Did your mother fight?"

"Yes, and wielded the small amount of magic she was given, but she was better with potions and medicines. There wasn't an ailment she could not treat, and she has passed down that knowledge to her children." He slid his hand up her arm, discovering the rest of her equally as cold.

"I would like to learn that as well."

"And you will." Vedikus peered at Aldora's exposed skin when another cold draft hit them. He blocked the worst of it. "Are you cold?"

"No."

"Your skin is frigid. Do not lie." Her smile faltered and she ran her palms over her arms, slowly at first, then with increasing speed.

"I'm not cold at all," she whispered hoarsely and

turned away. "I'm not cold, but I don't feel the warmth of my hands." She grasped his and then felt his skin. "I don't feel your heat either. Vedikus..." Her eyes widened with fear.

He pulled her into his arms and cupped the back of her head, feeling her breaths fan his chest. "We will make camp and cure you this night. I do not wish to wait another day in case you lose something else tomorrow." Aldora sagged against him and he pressed his nose into her hair, filling his nostrils with her female scent.

"I didn't even notice." She shook.

"The temperature is dropping and will continue to do so as we ascend the mountain path. You will notice it soon." The way was rife with traps and boulders to climb. Vedikus rubbed a piece of her shift between his fingers. "Come now, we've made back some time this day, and there are stores stashed nearby." He kept her in the crook of his arm as he passed the marker adorned with skulls and horns sculpted of stone. The bones piled at the bottom scattered with his hooves.

They quickened their steps, the cold bite of nightfall chewing at their heels as they crossed into Bathyr lands. It would be too much to hope for one of his brothers to be guarding this location seeing as they continuously traveled the paths, but he came across fresh tracks leading away. They were unhurried so he paid them no mind, his thoughts entirely on Aldora's well-being.

The cliffs rose up around them, blocking out the worst of the wind. Vedikus veered to a nearby secret path that overlooked the trail. He had Aldora climb up first and wait for him at the top of the narrow path up a fissure. They were shielded on all sides by rocks and shrubbery, with a look out and ambush point beneath them if anything were to pass the marker. A quick death by impalement would be too good for any trespasser.

He let Aldora catch her breath and take in the view as he headed into a crevasse in the wall, turning his head so his horns would not scrape the stone. Inside lay a small pit with enough supplies to last a day. Vedikus checked for new traps and enchantments before starting the fire.

He heard Aldora come in and sit by his side while he unearthed a clay jug of water from within which he placed atop the embers to bring to a boil.

"Will this hurt?" she asked softly.

"I don't know."

"How come? I thought your mother—"

"We were not told everything. I would have preferred to wait until we were farther up the mountain but I will not linger now that we're well outside of Prayer's boundaries."

"Maybe it is for the best that I have lost the sensation of touch," she admitted, pinching her arm. "Funny thing is… every time I have lost something of myself, the only memory I have left of it is of you. The way you smelled that first night, the feel of you. It's the only thing that remains after everything else is lost. I can't remember apples and I've eaten them my whole life. I just know that they are sweet and tart but all I imagine is fire and sweat." Aldora lifted on her knees and traced one finger along his horn.

"I'm honored," he said.

"It wasn't by choice."

"And yet you have allowed me to fill you in every way

229

that matters. If you weren't in threat of your health, your life, then I would consider leaving you to be consumed by me. It is how it should be," he grunted, putting some of the stored herbs into the water to help freshen it and ease Aldora's throat when she drinks. "Regardless, you will have nothing in your future but me."

"And you? Would you consume yourself with me?"

His hands clenched. "Do not make me give voice to my weaknesses."

She sat back and withdrew her hand. "If I am a weakness then I am pleased," she chuckled. "Weaknesses are the sole focus of a dedicated warrior."

Her words rang in his skull. Vedikus watched as the water bubbled up from the tapered spout of the jug and pour into the fire, sizzling and steaming the small space.

"What do you," he took the jug off the fire and let it cool, finding it hard to voice his question, "think of me?" He had the urge to press her into the ground and force answers from her lips, to taste them with his own even if it was not what he wanted to hear. Aldora canted her head and removed her boots. Wiggling her toes, she brought her gaze back to his.

"You're my strength, minotaur, you could never be my weakness."

Vedikus narrowed his eyes although her words made his chest tight. His strength was his most prized attribute. He had honed it since before he could utter a word, fighting with his brothers before he knew what a weapon was. By the time he could use a blade, he no longer needed it in his arsenal to defeat an opponent; his muscles were enough to take down any beast. His horns sharpened to gore any in his way.

"You care for me, female?"

He cherished Aldora's lighthearted nature, and when she bowed her head and hid her growing smile under her hair, his fingers ached to brush the strands aside to see it.

"I can't rely on my own power to survive here," she said. "It was hard for me to understand that, but since we left Prayer… you could have hurt me for speaking to Calavia alone but you didn't. You didn't. You listened to me, and I'm more sorry about how you would react than I was when I was seeking to save myself. Call it magic, or the darkness of this place, but I care for you."

He watched her idly pluck at her shift. "You have learned the hardest lesson there is to learn about living in this cursed place." Vedikus pushed her hair back to reveal her face. "We do what we must to survive. There is no living beast or human who is not afflicted."

Aldora grasped his wrist when he pulled back, bringing it to her cheek. "It's not just those who are here but those on the other side who are equally affected." She shuddered and he caressed his thumb over her skin. "I'm glad I was journeying home when I was, when I heard your voice. I blamed you at first for everything, but know now that it may have been fate."

Fate. Vedikus rose to stand, pulling Aldora up with him. "What are we doing?" she asked.

He led her from the small cave and back out into the open. "I want to show you fate." Vedikus searched the roiling, shrouded sky looking for the tiny bright orb of the rising moon. The mountain breeze curled the mist in spinning swirls overhead but he caught a glimpse among the clouds and pointed. "Do you see the moon?"

"Yes."

"It was watching us that night." But that was not why he showed it to her now. "The history of my people says we were born under a moonlit night. It was said that the first of our kind ruled the labyrinth, eons ago. She was the queen of all the winding paths and hedges that were meant to mislead others but she was trapped within, lost, because she could not leave it, and she was feared. The world feared her and her domain because it could not be claimed, though many had tried.

"There was a king who claimed the bull's lands, the giant maze, and built his kingdom around it. The queen, stuck within, could do nothing but grow in hatred toward this weak man who dared to own such a magical place, and so, for years, she killed all who dared to trespass, and with her loneliness and anger, her kingdom grew. The walls split and expanded and rose from the dirt, and what was once peaceful in the daylight had become tainted."

"Is this... Is this truth?" Aldora asked.

"It is truth to the minotaur. We are all descended from the first, under the guise of the moon. Come." Vedikus led her back inside when the moon vanished overheard and the night deepened. He stoked the fire, and with a little bit of water, cleaned root stores to feed Aldora. When she was done eating, he handed her the wax vial from his pouch. She took it carefully and clutched it to her chest.

"What happened next in the story?"

Vedikus unsheathed his axes and placed them safely away. "The king sent men to stop the bull. Many, in fact, but none returned, and with each new attack, the labyrinth grew, and with it, the queen lost what little peace she had left. Eventually, the king retreated because his lands, and even his people had been taken from him. Those that still followed him, followed with renewed fear of the place and it became something to avoid. In a final effort, they brought fires to the labyrinth to burn it down. That night, under the moon, his castle succumbed to the magic and the queen came for him. She had trapped him like he had tried to trap her."

"Why didn't the king flee?"

"He was a warlord and refused to be defeated. Men who have had power cannot easily relinquish it when there is still a chance to fight to keep it."

Aldora peered at him curiously. "I would have fled, rallied, and then returned with a plan."

"Would you have gotten into his situation to begin with?"

She hummed and pursed her lips. "No. I wouldn't. I was always best at hiding. I would not make a great queen."

"It is good you are not a character in this story then, female. Those who lead cannot hide."

"I agree. The current king of Savadon does not hide…" She trailed off. "He is not a good man."

"Rulers rarely are," he agreed. "My sire was chief of our old tribe and was not liked by many. We followed him because we respected and feared him; he was the best warrior among all minotaur and no one, not even his sons, could best him in battle. He was more bull than man and those animalistic traits were apparent for all to see. You have feet where I have hooves, you have straight legs where mine are bent, but my father had more for his parents were both minotaurs. My mother could not kiss my sire for his face was not human. I was born with more of my mother in my appearance than my sire."

"Your family does not all look the same?"

"We are all minotaurs but our differences are easily discerned. Do all of your family members have brown eyes?"

"I—" she started and stopped. "I can't remember. I believe we all do. Why?"

"My mother had blue eyes," he said.

"And yours are black. It is the same for humans. We do not all look alike."

"Hmm…"

Vedikus lifted the jug and checked the temperature of the water with his finger. It was cool enough to drink and he offered it to her. "Use this to wash that down." He indicated the vial. Aldora placed the water by her knee, taking a deep breath.

"I'm afraid."

The light of the fire cast her soft features in gold and shadows. Her smile had faded and her expression grew pensive. He missed the quiet moment they shared now that it had passed. *I do not want this to end.* She looked at the medicine in her hand as if it were the only thing left in the world.

"Do not be, I checked it for ill magic and ingredients. The hag of Prayer would not offer you false goods for fear of bringing the Bathyr into her lands." The hag would be dealt with, but in what way depended on her.

"She does not like chaos," Aldora muttered.

"Sometimes it can't be avoided."

"Will you distract me while I take it?"

Confusion filled his head at her request. *Distract her?* Vedikus longed to have her sheathing his bull's cock again, longed to expel the new seed his loins had created to breed her with, but to do so while she took the cure? He shook his head, his voice gruff and deep. "How?"

"Finish the story."

The strain in his thighs eased slightly although his shaft remained semi-hard and twitchy. A tendril of steam escaped his nostrils. Vedikus tilted his head and forced the tension from his chest. He was not good at taking orders but he could not deny her. He licked his lips and nodded, reaching for one of his axes to trace his fingers along the blade.

"The king knew he had been defeated and that he had no choice but to face her in battle. The queen had all but won and the only victory left was to kill the leader of her enemies. She had him where she wanted him, but when the time came to gore his body, she could not do it."

Aldora uncorked the top of the vial and sniffed the liquid, sighing quietly as her other hand rested on the clay jug.

"Be glad that you cannot smell it," he paused. "It will be easier that way."

"Is it that bad?"

"It's not pleasant."

She nodded.

"What was her life before the king came into it?" Vedikus continued after a moment, wishing he had more control of the situation. "She resided in a small world, alone, waiting each day for her enemy to attack her lands, but what would she do when it was over? The queen could not live with such a fate now that she knew there was more than just her labyrinth and its magic, so she offered the king a deal: his life and kingdom for a child."

Aldora met his eyes and raised the vial again, posing it at her lips. He leaned forward, letting the axe go limp in his hand. The evening light faded to a deep grey, darkening the entrance of the cave, and the sounds of night critters sounded among the crackle of the fire.

"Did he accept?" she asked instead of swallowing.

"In awe of the queen, he did, but it was not at all what he had expected. The king was never able to leave the labyrinth with what the queen bestowed upon him, his rule was no longer over the land of light, of mere human men, but of all that resides in the maze he so desperately tried to conquer."

She stiffened, inhaled, and tipped her head back, drinking the contents in one go. Vedikus leaned back, waiting for something to happen. Aldora dropped her hand and placed the empty waxen cylinder aside while rubbing her mouth. He indicated the water and she turned her attention to it, taking several deep swallows until there was nothing left.

"How do you feel?"

She rubbed her hands together curiously. "Nothing. I feel nothing. I wish I knew what to expect…"

"Expect it to work," he reassured, reaching for her. Vedikus pulled her into his lap and pressed her head back against his chest, resting his chin atop it. "Rest now. I will guard your sleep." She settled against him and he wrapped his arms around her, sealing her within the shell of his large body. His nostrils flared as the sharp smell of magic filled his nose, mixed with her sweet scent. It relaxed him, reminding him of a time when he was young. When he and his brothers would curl up together when his mother told them stories. When he last had something besides responsibility and bloodshed in his life.

"I hope it works," she whispered, and he pressed his lips to her head.

"Hope is for the weak, female."

"That makes sense." Her voice softer still. "What happened next?"

Vedikus rested his back against the cave wall. "The first minotaur was born, not all bull nor all man, but with the abilities of both. The queen returned to her labyrinth with the babe, leaving the king to rule by himself in a desecrated castle of his own making. He resides there still, looking out over the world he would forever be trapped in, waiting, like all monsters here do." Aldora mumbled weakly and he caressed her skin, feeling sleep take her from him.

He turned his eyes to the wax vial, now partially melted by the fire, the pale wax pooling. He watched it until it lost all its shape and returned back to its original form, and after a long while Aldora began to shiver slightly in his arms. *Feeling*, once again.

Chapter Twenty

Aldora wakened, feeling cold, yet burning up at the same time. Her eyes snapped open to shadows and low light and the sounds of night filling her ears. Sweat drenched her clothes and she shifted, finding herself secure in an embrace forged from iron.

"Vedikus," she gasped, feeling his hold on her loosen enough to allow her to lift her head. "I'm... I think it's working." He squeezed her flesh as she met his eyes, not responding to her otherwise. "What's wrong?" She gasped again, her skin rising in gooseflesh as she studied his face. It was still night, the shadows still deep.

She closed her eyes and inhaled, suddenly overcome with the smell of smoke and earthy musk. *It worked.*

I can smell. She took several more lengthy breaths just to convince herself it was true.

I can taste it in the air. I can taste the smoke.

"Are you well?" A hand cupped her cheek, warming her face, and she nuzzled it, meeting his gaze. His voice was as low and enthralling as it was the first night she heard it. Her sex tightened in anticipation.

Without responding, she answered him by raising her lips to his. Softened by the silence and the enclosure of the cave, it was more of a lingering whisper, a touch of satin where she initiated. The feel of it filled her with excitement. His mouth moved under hers after a moment, responding with whispers of its own. She moaned, lapping at the taste of salt on the skin around his lips.

Hands moved up the back of her body, teasing like their tongues to lift her dress over her head. Aldora let out a short laugh when it caught around her long hair and she had to untangle herself from it. "Do not rip what I can't replace. Not again."

Vedikus grunted and pulled her back down to him, pressing her now-naked body to his. She moved her legs to straddle him, straightening on her knees to capture his mouth. The brief wonderment she'd felt was now gone, and she found herself battling the warrior minotaur once again. The kiss deepened and his hand came up to cup her head, holding her in place, forcing her acceptance. Aldora moaned and clutched him back, wanting more of his power.

His brutal seduction.

His tongue shot its way into her mouth, penetrating her, licking her teeth and rubbing against her own. Vedikus groaned and she felt its vibration straight to her core, strumming her desire.

He's in me. His voice, his name, him. Her sex clenched and the heat built, leaving her wanton with need. The sudden burst of his smell, his taste, his feel overpowered every fiber of her being. She ground her hips, seeking the hard feel of his monstrous shaft against her. Her world spun as his mouth brutalized hers, ravaging in its intent, reminding her that he held all the control.

That any choices she made were because he let her do so, not because she had any freedom, that no longer bothered her. Instead, it heightened her desire.

Aldora dug her nails into his chest, feeling the coarse yet smooth feel of scars under her fingertips. She rubbed her sex over his leathers, covering it with her essence, and slicking the velvet feel of it. Her body begged for more.

I can't. A murmur of desperation sounded from her and Vedikus pulled back, leaving her mouth well and truly raw. Her nails grazed down his skin as she sought to dislodge his heavy loincloth and remove the last of the barriers between them. When she felt his bulge, it was already dripping with lubrication, and a deep groan filled her ears. Aldora closed her eyes when clutched his wet shaft. *So large.*

"It takes no small amount of courage for a small thing like you to take a bull's cock in hand," his voice teased her.

"It takes no courage at all." She squeezed him again.

"Is that so, female?" His eyes twinkled with mischief.

"None at all."

"Then show me how courageous you really are."

Aldora straddled his velvet thighs and pressed forward to steal a kiss. A brief graze of teeth. Her hand slipped down his engorged length to knead his root. She nipped his flesh as his hands fisted into her hair, making her eyes water. She moved her hand lower still and found his massive testicles, knowing from past experience that it drove men mad, and cupped them in her hand.

Vedikus arched up into her with a roar, stabbing her sex with his prick. She moaned loudly, removing her hand while the sound echoed. His chest puffed out, his muscles tensed, and a gush of steam poured from his mouth. Aldora breathed in the heat, pulling more of his power inside her. It burned her throat.

"I can do more."

His back hit the wall. "It may kill me, female." She rolled his testicles between her hands, urged on by the glaze of need in his eyes. *Inside me.* Her sex clenched around nothing.

"Are you so easily felled?"

One hand palmed her hip. "You say that as you milk me for my seed," he groaned. "Any beast would be lame to fight such a precarious position. You could maim me in one sure stroke."

"Then I have found your one other weakness," Aldora warned with a small smile. Vedikus pulled her back down onto him by her hair. His other hand came up to cup her sex, and calloused thick fingers slipped through her folds. Vedikus rubbed vigorously. Her smile faded. His fingers circled her entrance and spread her wetness down her thighs. She released his root and gripped his shoulders, leaning forward to rest her brow on them.

"And I have found yours," Vedikus threatened her ear, one finger surging up inside her, forcing her hips in the air. "You tease me and I allow it, female, because you have become special to me, but you play with blades. I will use every weapon in my grasp to become the victor, and this," his hand pistoned, driving her hips up further as he pushed another his finger inside her, "is a weakness I will exploit."

"Yes," Aldora cried out, shuddering, wet all over. He thrust a third large finger in her, forcing her to take it. There was a stab of pain and she whimpered, biting down on her tongue. He touched a sensitive spot within and her muscles spasmed. Aldora gasped. Her legs trembled and the ground chaffed her knees.

"Daily, relentlessly, and without rest. You will fill my stable, Aldora."

Yes!

Vedikus chuckled, the sound wicked. He widened his fingers and stretched her, and returning her pain. Her teeth grazed his skin, her tongue tasting his flesh, gnawing with desperation as the first spark of bliss knotted her insides.

Aldora moved her toes under her and lifted up with a scream, pulling away with pleasurable shock. An orgasm tore its way out of her, clawing her senses to ruin. Her brow dampened with sweat as she twisted and fought her way off Vedikus's hand, the sudden rush of having her senses returned making her desperate. He grunted and rounded her body with his arm, bringing her back to him.

"Don't make me beg."

She barely heard it as she squirmed and caught her breath. He continued to ram his fingers inside her swollen sex, making her sacrifice more for him.

Aldora swallowed, and with a slurp, he released her with another chilling laugh. His hands grabbed her hips and lowered her upon him. She whimpered when the head of his bulge found her aching sex and sought to fill it. She reached up weakly and held onto his horns.

She pushed down onto him, her sex still constricting

from her orgasm, and winced. He watched her efforts with a twitching smile, groaning against her struggles. Aldora shot up then slid a little more back down, mounting him. She slumped against his chest when she was fully seated, finally filled. His fingers bit into her, leveraging her final impalement, and her perfect surrender.

I need more. She moved weakly. Vedikus lifted her on his bull's cock as if he heard her thoughts, thrusting her back down. Another scream left her lips as she felt her insides being rearranged, the pain intense, but the pleasure exploded like a wildfire from it. She melted as he moved her above him.

Aldora threw her head back and lifted her face to the ceiling, filling the cave with frenzied moans and grunts as she rode her minotaur hard, being led by his groping hands, giving herself to her senses. Their flesh slapped and the fire died to completion at her back, pitching them into darkness. Another knot began to untie within her core and she pressed her fingers to her clit, rubbing it in wild circles, taking it in.

Thunder and scalding rain filled her, shooting up inside, while the source jostled her above him. A ringing sounded in her head as his seed shot from his tip, implanting in her womb. She rode him back down to the floor as Vedikus continued to spurt inside her until seed gushed from her sex to coat their thighs. Her fingers stroked her clit frantically.

He ripped her hand away and replaced it with his own, violently bringing her back over the edge. The noises she made sounded inhuman and garbled but she didn't care, couldn't even muster the strength to discern if they were even hers, having lost herself in release.

Vedikus twisted her to the floor, spreading her legs wide, as he continued to pump, as if he couldn't get enough of her body's jerking orgasm, and every time she constricted around him, the tips of his horns scrapped the stone above her head. Aldora settled back, panting from exertion as her bull bred her, and she allowed it, feeling her desperation vanish and her excitement return.

The first threads of dawn peeked through the small, jagged entrance to the cave when Vedikus eased himself from her with a grunt, his body coming back down to plaster against hers. He rested his head in the crook of her shoulder, tickling her skin. He licked her, moving his tongue over her throat, along her jaw, and to her forehead. Aldora shivered despite her exhaustion and felt the soft tapping of his tail caressing the side of her thigh.

"Vedikus," she moaned softly. His tongue slid from her face and moved down her body, cleaning her, and tasting her everywhere. If there was ever a moment where she may have liked being numb with illness, it was quickly expelled from her head. Her limbs fell lifelessly away from her body as he worked his mouth over them.

When it was over, she sighed with contentment and watched, languid and sated, as he rose naked above her and eyed her lifeless body with possession. Power emanated from him, addictive power that made her want to crawl on her hands and knees and worship at his cloven feet. Aldora stretched, hiding the thrill of her thoughts. His seed gushed out of her.

"Do not move," he ordered before picking up the jug

and leaving the cave with his tail swinging. She stared at the point where he had vanished, disturbed with how lonely she abruptly felt out of his presence. Her toes curled nervously as she tried to rest, and tried to obey.

He returned sometime later, rousing her, with fresh wood and a dead creature. She watched, moving to lie on her side, as their fire was built back up and a less humid warmth replaced the heat from their rutting. Light returned to their stony bubble, and with it, the prospect of a new day.

Aldora rose up and pulled her shift to her.

"I prefer you bare."

She bunched the fabric in her hands. "I would like to dress."

"Then dress." He cocked his head, his eyes pinning her. She twitched nervously and waited for him to look away. He didn't. The fire crackled.

Aldora straightened to meet the challenge and lifted her arms above her head, showing off her nakedness for one unhindered, taunting second longer before slipping her shift on. With it in place, she still felt naked under his gaze. *Because I still am, under this...*

He snorted once and shifted his focus back to his kill, taking her dagger out to skin it. Aldora noticed his prick stiffen again before she looked away, her attention returning to the overwhelming amount of wetness between her legs. She searched for something to clean herself but gave up after a moment when she remembered how very little they had now after Prayer.

Vedikus made short work of the carcass, disposing the excess well away from the cave, and cleaning it.

"What is that?" she asked just to fill the quiet.

"A mountain tark. They are common here in the cliffs and more so as we ascend. They're called to the heights and are often found high up in trees if they make their way out of this region." He stuck it on the blade of her weapon and placed it in the fire, next to the jar that was boiling over with water. Before long, the smell of meat being roasted sent her stomach rumbling. She had eaten little in the last span of days, and she was beginning to feel it.

"Come." Vedikus pulled apart sizzling strips of meat with his fingers. She moved to his side at his bidding, and with the same possessive look he gave her earlier, he fed her from his hand. Aldora chewed slowly and brushed her hair with her fingers.

"Vedikus," she started, unsure, between bites, still feeling the wetness from their coupling every time she shifted her legs.

"What?"

"Why do you ask me to mount you?" Aldora blurted out quickly.

He glanced at her sharply before cutting off another strip. "It is a tradition among my people to claim our mate."

She scrunched her face in confusion.

"Our strength comes from the animalistic side, but our power comes from our lineage with humans and the purity of our blood. When a bull mates, they mount the female, and we are driven to do the same, but sex is often had between the different clans of a tribe. We see our ancestors as greater than us because they have lived and have propagated, but it stems from the natural wrongness of the act itself. A female cannot mount a bull, it is not done, but we are human too and choose to protect that part of ourselves that the queen has given us. To have you mount me," Vedikus lowered the dagger, "is a devious act and one not followed by many minotaurs. It binds us. It is not done unless it is between two who choose to mate for life because it wars with our instincts. For you to lower yourself onto me," his voice deepened, "proves the union is sought... not forced."

Her mouth dried up and she lifted the jug to clear the taste from her mouth. "I didn't know. Does that mean we are married?"

"That is a human concept and one I have heard about. Yes, in vagueness, we are married but there is no way to break the bind which we have placed. That *I* have placed."

Her belly fluttered. Aldora wiped the back of her hand across her mouth and hid a small smile behind it. *Trickery, again.* She knew she should be irate, but such small things no longer mattered to her. A small piece of her knew she would have stayed the moment he bound her in rope to his side. That same part wanted to show her appreciation because she wanted her monstrous warrior, needed him in the quietness of her heart.

The thing I feared most...
The labyrinth.

It had become an otherworldly salvation. A dangerous one, but there hadn't been a day in all the long years of residing in Thetras and working on the farm that her life hadn't been in danger, that the corrupt, paranoid, deviant men and women of Savadon hadn't oppressed her.

"So... we are mated," she whispered to herself.

Vedikus's gaze sharpened on her further, heating up her insides. "Yes, we are mated."

She no longer hid her smile, overcome with a wonderful sense of freedom, and climbed back into his lap. He stiffened, unsure, as she settled over him, reaching down to move his leathers to the side once again to find his erect prick. Without meeting his eyes, she took him back into her body with a sigh and leaned into his chest. His hands came up to wrap back around her, holding her to him. "You do not know what you do, female," his voice was raspy and thick above her.

"I know exactly what I'm doing." Aldora rested her head upon him and closed her eyes. "This time I know what it means."

I know you.

She pressed her lips to his skin and tasted his flesh, inhaling heavily to take in his scent at the same time. There was little energy left in her bones to move as she drowned in his heady aura, his enchanting voice, and his heat.

Vedikus leaned back and pulled her atop him, keeping them joined. Aldora matched her breathing to his, and with the early morning light brightening to day, she found true rest for the first time since she could remember, well away from all that she had known. The past she no longer wanted to dwell on. Because right at that moment…

She felt like a queen.

Chapter Twenty-One

The sun was bright through the mist when they finally left the cave. Vedikus tilted his head to the sky, enjoying the small amount of warmth he got from it. His clan had chosen the mountains near Prayer for many reasons, but climate and defensibility were among them. The elevation lessened the mist to a point and sometimes when least expected, one could see the sky in all its glory.

It brought him comfort. The secretive moments when the world cleared, and when he and his brothers first struck their weapons into the cliffs above, they all knew they had found the land the Bathyr would settle.

"I thought I would never see it again," Aldora said next to him. "It's even more beautiful than I remembered."

"When we reach our destination, it will only get better." And he looked forward to showing her. "My brothers will know by now that we are ascending. They will be waiting if they do not meet us halfway."

"How?"

Vedikus watched as the glow of the sun vanished behind stringy clouds, and when it was gone, he faced Aldora who continued to look up at the misty sky. He took her chin, turning her eyes to him. "Keep your eyes on me. I will not lead you astray." She nodded mutely and he released her, still jealous of the sky. "As for my brothers, there are three guarding our home. They maintain traps and enchantments that have been placed among the pathways and caves here. The moment we crossed the marker would be when they were alerted, however, I know the locations of all of the traps."

"Just three?" Aldora frowned. "I thought… I thought when you said tribe, that there would be more."

They resumed walking and he felt her hand tug on the back of his loincloth. He grunted to himself, pleased that she still sought his assistance.

"There are only five of us currently," he said, hollowly, "We left the main tribe several seasons ago…"

"Wait!" She jerked his cloth back, and he had to stop from being unclothed entirely. "Please," she added quickly, softening her hold. Vedikus reached up and smoothed the hair out of her face where the wind whipped it.

"You do not have to fear me, female," he gritted his teeth, angered he even had to say it. "I would never unleash my violence on you. We are one now." Even the thought made him furious. What point was there in going through the trouble for a human mate to just hurt them? He did not want what his sire and mother had.

Aldora reached up and pulled back her hair harshly, revealing her wide, worried eyes. "It's not that. I don't know what to expect anymore. I thought we journeyed to

252

a-a settlement of some sort, with well, many minotaurs, not just three."

"Five," he corrected.

"Five then. There's so few. Why are there so few of you?"

So few...

His chest constricted tightly as he searched her gaze. It implored him to answer, but to answer would be speaking the words of his brother's plight and bringing it to light. The Bathyr never spoke of the incident that shattered their loyalty to their mother tribe, and he found it hard to try. The words tasted bitter.

She is Bathyr. She has a right to know.

Vedikus grunted, forcing the words to rise. "We are few because our old tribe betrayed us. They thought it within their power to sour the name of my mother." He pulled her against him when the wind shrieked, rubbing her bare arms with his large ones to warm her.

"Your mother is alive?" Aldora pushed against his chest. "I thought—"

"She is gone."

"Gone?"

"Come and I'll tell you another story to pass the time." He tucked her under his arm and they continued their climb. "Those that await us are my blood brothers, the only bulls my mother and father sired. The Bathyr." It was not often he heard his ancestral name aloud.

"Steelslash was my sire's name, changed for what he did best, a warrior unlike any living minotaur had seen. He became chief when he returned from the barrier paths with my mother many years ago in hope that his prowess would breed well with human blood. His power was a beacon for my kind, and the minotaur followed him blindly, lured by it, to parts of the world we sought to conquer."

"You speak of them as if they are in the past... I'm sorry for your loss," Aldora said, startling him. *She is sorry for me?* "In a way... I've lost my parents—my family—too," her voice softened. "But knowing they are still out there, alive, settled in a good life, eases my pain."

"It would ease mine as well."

"I am your family now, Vedikus," she breathed.

He barely heard her words through the wind. *Family. My mate readily accepts her fate.* His heart beat hard within his chest, and he leaned his nose to the top of her head so he could breathe her comforting scent in. His senses flooded with sweet evergreen, and his tail thumped under his loincloth. "Yes," he rasped. "You are Bathyr, and you'll give our clan a way to become the mightiest tribe this land has ever birthed." Her fingers pressed into his skin and caressed one of his many scars.

"It's given me hope—" she started.

Hope.

"And a strange sort of excitement."

Vedikus snorted, and released some of the built up steam in his chest, helping Aldora over a steep, mossy rise. Before long, the boulders that littered the rocky paths were replaced with shrubs, and as they crested the first summit, giant black trees met them for the final ascent. Aldora gasped, and he pressed her closer to him. He refused to look at the trees directly because of their ominous sight, like dozens of dark needles impaling exposed flesh.

They are our greatest defense. Even if his brothers didn't agree.

But to walk among them was like walking through his home now, even when the mist darkened them to jagged teeth. Blood red markers appeared on the trees ahead in his periphery, all painted seasons past by his clan as a final line of warning.

His eye caught something else... Fresh footprints leading back the way they came.

Vedikus released Aldora and turned to see them end at the rocky path down below, but the shape and indent of them were unmistakable. They were the footprints of one of his kin, and fresh. His eyes narrowed on them.

"What's wrong?" Aldora asked, moving back against his side where her shivers lessened.

"One of my brothers passed through here recently, descending down to the paths we had just walked."

"But we saw no one, nor heard anything but the wind?" Her head moved as she took in the unshrouded area around them. "Right?"

Vedikus leaned down briefly to smell the soil. His nose twitched, but he found no traces of magic. *Why has my brother not sought us out?* "They must have been made during the night," he mumbled, straightening.

"Then we may have missed them when..." Aldora trailed off, a blush forming on her cheeks.

"Yes," he said with the sudden need to investigate further. Vedikus folded Aldora back into his embrace as a reminder that he had far more important things to take of. *There will be a reason, but it will have to wait.* "Let us continue, we are not far away now, and I would like to have you in my furs before the light begins to fade."

"Are you sure? If this is important, we can follow his tracks."

"No. You are cold and vastly under-equipped now for residing these lands. Let us go home."

"Then we will come back prepared and find our answers."

Vedikus grunted in agreement, settling one hand on his battle axe. The crunch of dead leaves sounded as they made their way up the steep cliff, following the tracks all the way to the top until they faded and were lost when dirt returned to rock. Aldora's breathing grew more hoarse and labored with each minute that passed, regardless of how much he helped her.

It did not sit well with him that one of his brothers might have gone past their camp the night before, knowing that it was a well-used one among the Bathyr during long scouting trips. The enchantments placed would have alerted the entire clan of its disturbance, like a tiny prick to the back of his neck. When the magic sparked, it had a distinct feeling, unmistakable like its smell. He did not know one of his brothers who would pass a clan member by. *The human with me is enough to put the Bathyr on high alert. Her scent will permeate the air.*

Aldora interrupted his thoughts, inhaling as she spoke. "Will you tell me more about your brothers?" Sweat glistened her brow, and parts of her loose dress clung despite the chill. "Will they expect much from me?"

"Only your contribution and your strength of will because that is what I expect. They will take you in as one of their own because you are mine. Do not worry what they think nor want, that is not your concern, nor should it ever be."

"But you were kicked out of your last tribe, I do not want the same to happen to me. I don't think I could live through another journey through this labyrinth."

Vedikus looked at her idly. "We were not kicked out, we left at our own accord."

"You have not said why…"

His hand squeezed the shaft of his weapon as the words burned his throat. *She deserves to know.* He had no qualm about Aldora knowing his past, even if it could hurt his kind. Like all beasts in this place, secrets were kept close, and minotaurs had little to no weaknesses as is. He knew she would not tell another monster, if only because he would never allow Aldora outside the realm of his control.

"When Steelslash brought my mother home, he brought something else with him as well. Something unseen and dangerous. The elders of the tribe did not know of it until many years later, and whether it was their chief that was responsible or my mother, is lost to history despite my brothers' and my best efforts."

"Worse than the mists?"

"Yes. During the reign of my sire, our tribe was unstoppable, nomadic, and we traveled the dead lands victoriously for many years. The dead lands are where the minotaur come from, the world which was consumed by the mists eons ago, deep inland, where there is nothing but old paths, crumbling ruins, and giants that roam unhindered. It is a different way of life from that led near humanity. We were hundreds strong when I was birthed, and with two hands, and two horns, we all carried more weapons than the average being.

"My mother was the first human brought back to us in over a century. The last was a human man who was mated with a female. He died before I was born. Once, I have been told, there had been dozens who lived among us in the past, but as the world changed and my kind did not move closer to the land of humans, they all but died out. The blood among us weakened greatly, and in turn, the mists closed in. As the years passed, we became more animalistic, digressing back to the creatures we were before."

"Arriving with your mother must have been a big deal…" Aldora shifted nervously at his side.

"Yes. It gave them *hope*." Vedikus spat out the word, hating it. He focused on his female's scent and the soft feel of her against him until his hate slipped away. "Hope that history would replay, and it did, for a time." They came upon a plateau that looked out over the lands that lay between them in those he spoke about. Those that lay beyond the expanse of mountains that took weeks to traverse. Those where his old tribe still roamed, even to this day. "There is nothing worse than false hope."

"I have hope, Vedikus. Someday I will teach you that it isn't so bad. You took away mine for a single moment, and that feeling," she paused and swallowed, "was frightening, but then you replaced it, and now… It's nearly all I feel. It does not feel bad."

"It's trickery," he argued. "It's a quiet lie."

"But why work so hard to stay alive in this desolate

place without it? You feel it even if you won't accept it. You told me it was only our strength and our knowledge that supplies you with the ability to survive here, but why work so hard for something if there is no end-goal in mind? We would all be nothing but thralls if true hope was lost."

He grunted. "Willpower and tenacity, proof of one's worth, loyalty and the ability to kill, to feed, have nothing to do with such an emotion. Hope is the labyrinth's greatest curse, not the mist. That dangling thread has killed more of my kind than any centaur assault or goblin trap." The airy brume swirled and shifted across the land-scape as if it heard him. Vedikus turned, bringing Aldora with him as they moved toward a hidden path along the cliff-face behind boulders that had been placed seasons ago. He glanced up and pointed to several others above. "You see those rocks? They are made to fall on those who find this path. If you are ever here without me, do not try and walk through the bushes, but follow the edge instead, they will not fall if you know where to step. I will not lose you to carelessness."

She nodded and placed her feet where his were a moment before, following his movements. "You may be right but I do not believe it. If it takes the rest of my life, I will change your mind. Hope is the only truth," she said with conviction.

His lips lifted. "I will look forward to you trying every day."

"You say that now," she laughed softly. "So it was hope that your father brought to your tribe. I do not see how that would lead to you and your brothers leaving."

"Steelslash did bring hope, but that was not what I was

speaking of, female. He brought ruin." The memories rose up like poisonous weeds in his skull. "He brought with him infertility, or so he was accused of many years later. During his reign, the only female who was able to conceive was my mother, and those who were heavy with child when they returned, all lost them before their birth. The babies just died without cause, and as this continued throughout his years leading, with my brothers being the only young of our tribe, the power he had so deftly built faded to resentment and paranoia. The Bathyr were looked upon with anger, my brothers and I were at once fought over by the other clans as studs, thinking we would cure our infertility but also as enemies. We had been born with gifts the others had not, and as we grew to adulthood, we found ourselves unbeatable. We became the tribes greatest warriors, but also their greatest threat."

Vedikus paused and hoisted Aldora, helping her over a high rise to a larger path above. *The last road home.*

"They blamed you for this tragedy?" she asked.

When he pulled himself over the edge, digging his hooves into the rock, he saw the footprints from earlier and the last small woods that hid his home from the many fiends that flew the skies.

"We are close now," he said, holding her close to his chest where he wrapped his arms tightly around her, drawing out the cold of her flesh. "They thought my father made a pact to bring my mother back, they blamed him for their inability to propagate. It was not something that was ignored, and when my brothers and I aged and no new blood was available to take the places of the warriors we lost over the years, it became Steelslash's obsession to pursue battle, because without bulls to overpower his enemies, he raged easily. We were forced to settle.

"By doing so was his greatest mistake, for when the tribe stopped, they had nothing else to divert their attention. My flesh is rent with scars from those days, but it was what happened next that changed the fate of the Bathyr forever. Steelslash died, suddenly, and the tribe turned on my mother, assuming this had all happened because she was a witch. I was not nearby when they took her..."

"Took her where?" Aldora peered up at him, forehead furrowed.

"I do not know. None of us do. Some said she walked off with a broken heart and never returned, some say she killed herself, others insist she was killed, captured, lost, gone. My elder brother, Dezetus, seized power despite all the bloodshed, and even then, no one came forth with the truth. My mother would have never left, of that, we can be certain. Not when her mate's body was fresh. We buried his body without ritual and with much bloodshed among us. When it was apparent no answers would be forthcoming, Dezetus suggested we leave. In turn, the Bathyr abandoned their tribe to whatever fate they forged, without their best warriors. It was the only way to stop the needless killing, the fighting, and now we live to build a new tribe, a dynasty that would rule these lands with iron hooves and sharpened blades." He smelled smoke and hints of cooked meat in the air. "If there was one way to stop the infertility of our female minotaur, it was through human blood."

"Me..."

"Yes."

"What if I can't?" Her eyes widened, and her hands left him to land on her belly.

"You are not afflicted with whatever has fallen upon my people. We have lost the old ways, and our gods are watching. I was not looking for a human, female or otherwise, when you heard me, but scouting and honing my strength for the time when we were ready. But fate had another idea, and it is time to stop preparing and to start rebuilding." As he said it, the large, black, wooden fence appeared through the trees that bordered up to the craggy walls of the mountain. Upon first glance, there appeared to be no gate within the matte black facade. "Come and be at ease for we have arrived."

Aldora pulled away from him and dropped her hands, gazing at the barrier before them. Vedikus felt a devious smirk twitch his lips, but did not let her see it. These walls were not unlike those that kept the mists inside, but without vines and growth, without footholds and places to clutch for climbing. *We are on the same side this time, female.* His prick thickened under his loincloth. His weariness faded.

"I'm nervous," she admitted, lifting one hand to her mouth.

"Then you are feeling what we want all trespassers and those who are brought here to feel. Know, from this point on, all strangers who look upon your home will feel the same."

Vedikus breathed deeply, taking in the smoke that was thicker here, already picturing the cooking fires inside his head, picturing his home, his trophies of past kills, and weapons he had either collected or made hanging on the walls of his den. *I see Aldora among them. She will be impressed with my prowess, not fear it.*

He wanted the awed look in her eyes when he showed off his skulls. He wanted the same look on her face when he ravaged her before them.

He lifted his head and roared, stamping his hoof in greeting. No one returned the call.

"Wait here," he said, unsheathing his weapons and approaching the hidden gate. It was sealed tight. He studied the wood but found no markings nor any other traces of tampering. He neither smelled blood or bile or rot either, and he searched for a hint of it in the wind.

"I have returned!" Vedikus called out again, stepping back.

This time a call was returned. "Hold!"

He narrowed his eyes and sheathed one of his weapons, turning to collect Aldora, but she was directly behind him with her dagger in hand. "You will not need that, female."

The gate *wooshed* open.

Aldora bent and slipped her weapon back into her boot, rising when a minotaur appeared at the gate. Her throat constricted despite the excitement coursing through her.

Will they accept me? Will they all be like Vedikus?

She did not think she could soften more than one warrior minotaur in her lifetime, let alone five. A morbid hope filled her at the prospect of more humans being brought here. Aldora buried the thought.

Her back stiffened when the minotaur approached.

He was bigger than Vedikus but only in height, with one horn broken at mid-point. It's midpoint broken off in smooth detail, making the scars of on his face even more pronounced. He was dressed the same as Vedikus, mostly naked but for a thick leather loincloth that covered his front and back, leaving the sides of his powerful thighs exposed. His legs and feet were also those of a bull's, but whereas Vedikus had a lighter appearance, this one had black fur with shoulder length hair to match upon his head. Part of his face was hidden behind it.

She reached up and gently placed her hand on Vedikus's arm, her heart settling at the touch.

"A human," the new minotaur rasped, stilling when his eyes landed on her.

"Her name is Aldora and she is your sister now. My mate."

The minotaur's mouth hardened which accentuated the rough markings of his flesh even more. *How could someone survive so much pain?* She rubbed her wrists.

"How?" Dezetus asked, his tone darkening.

"You demand answers after a long journey. We will speak later once we have settled. Aldora can not handle the cold like we can."

She glanced between the two minotaurs, noting their rigidity. *I'm not surprised.* At least she knew what to expect.

"Hail," she said with as much courage as she could muster.

Dezetus's frown deepened, and he did not greet her back. "Then settle and rest fast, for we have much to speak about and I have little taste for patience." He turned and stormed back through the gate.

Vedikus's snorted and re-sheathed his axe roughly. Aldora captured his free hand and tangled her fingers with his, walking with him through the eerie black gate. Beyond the barrier, she was shocked to find ruins—ruins that were not so different from her own world. The skeletal, gothic buildings were familiar to her. Their history apparent at first glance.

Remnants of Savadon.

Dezetus was nowhere to be seen.

"Where are the others?" she asked as Vedikus led her further in. They stopped short at one of the many buildings built into the rocks.

"Astegur is not here as you know, and unless he has returned before us, only Dezetus, Hinekur, and Thyrius are here standing guard. We are small, but not rash. I will see you inside before a new illness has a chance to take over where the last has been evicted." He pulled back a leather skin hanging in the entryway with an unusual pattern that she could not place and waited until she passed inside.

Light filtered through a stone opening above the arch of the door but from nowhere else. She stepped, and into what appeared to once be a home, long ago. Aldora wrapped her arms around herself as she made her way through the space. More light brightened her view when a second window was opened.

So human.

Her heart strummed, taking in the cryptic space, and accepting the fact that she felt like she belonged here where

Vedikus did not. His horns scrapped the ceiling in agreement.

The only thing that didn't feel entirely human was the decoration. Every wall in every room was covered in skins of monsters and animals that she had no name for, and some she shuddered to consider asking about. Despite the walls being covered, the only room that felt inhabited was the first. There was a stone oven built into the wall, and a single stool in the corner with whetstones and weapons lining the walls to its sides. In front of the oven was a large pile of furs she assumed was a bed.

Her mouth watered looking at it.

Relief flooded her senses.

"We spent the majority of our life as nomads and know little of keeping a home."

Aldora smiled. "This was once made by humans."

"Does it suit you?"

"More than you could know." She raised her gaze to meet his dark one. He hovered over her and invaded her space, and for a brief second, Aldora closed her eyes and let herself drown in his consuming presence. It comforted her.

Fire and brimstone flooded her nose as his hand grasped her hair, pulling it like he often did. Her shift was no protection at all from her minotaur.

"Thank you," she whispered, finding her palms sweaty, her fingers twitching. "Thank you…"

"For what, female?"

"For saving my life."

He leaned down and pressed his mouth to her shoulder, licking her skin. "The only one worth saving."

"How did you know?"

Vedikus tilted his head at her question. "Your voice. I needed to hear more of it, even if it killed me."

Her smile widened. Hope flared. "You are not as hard as you make yourself out to be, Minotaur. You would have killed yourself for an apple farmer. What would your brothers have thought if you had died?"

"That it was an honorable death. You will soon see when you meet them."

"I look forward to it."

He tugged her hair once before letting it go, picking her up to lie her upon his furs. She looked up at him with the same possessive expression he mirrored back. And with her dark captor filling her vision, her head, her heart, she was exactly where she belonged.

Epilogue

Aldora curled her arms over her middle and looked out over the cliffs. She was draped in new furs and skins, given to her by Vedikus straight from his walls.

I wear his conquests. She was pleased to do so, reveling in the strength of her mate. Her fingers drifted over the stitching she had put upon and ties that held them upon her body.

She had come here nearly every day since Vedikus showed her the hidden trails to this spot. The view was breathtaking. She couldn't quite explain what drew her to come back so frequently since it was more of the same endless ocean of gauzy white.

But she liked to watch the mist dance with the wind and shift with the sky. And sometimes, when the light from the sun was at its brightest, she could glimpse the cerulean blue skies beyond. Whenever that pop of blue filled her vision—for the moment that it lasted—she thought of her family and the farm. *We all have to leave the nest sometime.* She just wished she could have said a proper goodbye first.

Vedikus appeared at her side. "You are always here when I cannot find you."

She pressed her body to his, and his arm came up to enclose her in.

"Perhaps you should start by looking here first then. I like the mystery. I've always wondered about all that I can't see," she said idly, comforted. "Although most of the time I hope to catch a glimpse of the sky."

"Ah yes. The color is intriguing, brilliant within so much white. I have never seen it so clearly since bringing you here."

"Because I repel the mist? You should see the sky when there is nothing to obscure it, it goes on for an eternity. And at night it sparkles with stars."

"One day, when my brothers find their mates, it will open up for us at this peak and it will never close again. One day we will be free of this mist." His fist hit his chest. Aldora pressed her cheek to his side and nodded shallowly. She didn't know how she felt about other women coming here. There was a selfish place in her head that was looking forward to such a time, if it was just to be by someone of her own kind, who had survived the first night as a sacrifice.

There are others out there.

She wanted to save them all, but to want that also meant she accepted what the kingdom of light was doing. She did not want to become one of the many monsters ravenous for humans. Even if her intent was pure.

"I do not like you coming up here alone. There are

predators that fly these skies. You are safe among the trees where they will not see you, but up here, you're ripe for the plucking."

Aldora lifted her head to look at him. "Would you come after me if I was caught up?"

"Yes," he said it with such finality it made her pulse race. "Come." Vedikus pulled her away from the edge and toward the path. "We will see Dezetus off. He is at the gate as we speak."

She gave one last look over the mist, finding it had settled during their brief conversation. A little over a week had passed since she and Vedikus made it to his home. *Our home.* She had to remind herself. Bathyr. Aldora had named it such for her minotaur. A home that was three times the size of her previous one, now that she'd had the chance to explore properly. After the first several days of rest that was forced upon her, she had found herself horrendously bored and had taken it upon herself to clean out the ruins of all their dirt, overgrowth, and webbing, starting with her home. The labor was back-breaking, but it kept her busy while the others hunted and scouted. She would do more, but the tension was thick down below. Dezetus was not easy to get along with.

She found him stalking her, studying her as if she was an oddity far more than she was comfortable with. *I'm happy he's leaving.*

She followed Vedikus down the peak, making her way slowly over the rocky path, listening to the dirt and gravel crunch under his hooves. She was getting used to them. She had explored him thoroughly, going so far as washing his body from horn tip to boney hooves, taking her time and allowing herself to grow accustomed to their differences. At night, when she lay awake in the gloom, curled into her bull, Aldora could hear dual heartbeats under her ear.

One for the animal and one for the man. She listened for the sound now whenever they rested and relished the peace of mind that accompanied it.

A gust of wind blasted over her and she tugged her furs more securely around her frame.

Vedikus stood at the bottom of the path, where it changed from rocks to stone stairs, waiting for her. She licked some warmth back into her lips and closed the distance, taking his hand as he helped her down the last drop. His hand engulfed her own. Her nose twitched as she caught the smell of wood-burning smoke and the faded aroma of the morning meal.

"Thank you," she murmured, looking over the many stone buildings built into the mountain. Most of which remained untouched or impossible to get to from hundreds of years of deterioration. *Someday.* Her resolve hardened, and her curiosity piqued. Now that Dezetus was leaving, she would explore all that she'd wanted to when she'd been nervous to do so before.

Now, that she didn't have a lurker.

Vedikus grunted. Together, they descended an old staircase that zig-zagged down the cliff-face between several of the ghostly structures. Before long, they were hidden within the canopy of the trees.

Scattered about were worn carvings decorating the walls. Human depictions. Most she hadn't even begun to try to understand. After finding an elaborate, albeit barren, altar room within the first building that led up the way they came, she began to see this place as more of an ancient temple and less of an abandoned settlement. It reminded her of the temples in Thetras, but only in the severity of the embellishments to the decor.

Her awe of this place had grown into respect as she'd learned how the Bathyr lived and operated. *This wasn't a place for peasants. Or beasts with horns.* And yet both had ended up here regardless of its original intent.

They continued to walk in silence as they made their way to the gate and past the ruins that housed the altar and where the minotaur nested. No one met them for the whole journey.

Because the others were inexplicably gone.

Dezetus came into view, crouched next to the bonfire they all shared, with a dagger in one hand and a stray piece of wood in the other. A familiar shape was forming where parts of the wood were whittled away. Aldora paused, her eyes narrowing on the piece.

"I have been waiting," Dezetus said without looking up.

On me? Aldora looked away from his hands, to his broken horn, and stiffened.

"You have been waiting since our mother expelled you from her womb, and you will be waiting long after this day has come and gone," Vedikus grumbled as Dezetus stood.

Aldora took a step forward as a wall of minotaur blocked her view. They were large, far bigger than any human man, and far stronger. She looked at Vedikus. Her bruised thighs were proof of that strength through their

273

vigorous mating. She pressed her legs infinitesimally closer together.

"And you, brother, will stand by my side and wait with me, such is our curse." Dezetus's eyes landed on her. "The others should be here but have vanished the same day you arrived."

"They have not vanished, I tracked hoof prints halfway down the mountain. There were no signs of any other passage but our own from our ascent. There is no mist-beast trespassing our lands. No signs of an attack, ambush, nor fight and none of the enchantments we have placed have been triggered. If Hinekur and Thyrius left, it was not because of us, but because of you."

Dezetus kept his gaze on her despite her silence. He made her want to hide. "It matters not what you say, I will find the answers for myself," he said, his voice darkening with warning. A thin, almost imperceptible wisp of steam trailed from his nostrils, dissipating within the unkempt hair that fell heavily over his face. His irises were lighter in color than Vedikus's and startling among all the shadows that seemed to want to cling to him. Oftentimes, she thought he just looked... *broken*.

Vedikus gripped his brother's shoulder and the other minotaur finally tore his intense gaze away from her. "Then find them and turn your anger to something else," he hissed. Steam released from both of them as Vedikus knocked his horns against his brothers. "We are prepared to take over the next watch."

"*You* are prepared! Not her. You should not have brought her here without warning!" Dezetus raged, beating his horns roughly back.

Aldora moved away.

"She is my mate!"

"Do not forget what has happened in the past—"

"You think me weak enough to forget?" Vedikus placed his hands over the shafts of his axes.

"We have come here to find answers! To rebuild what was once great about our people, not to repeat history." Dezetus turned away and stormed to the gate. Her eyes widened as she watched him walk away. There was one large battle axe strapped across his bare back. She had never seen a weapon so large.

"And you think a gift of fate should be ignored?" Vedikus demanded.

"I did not receive this gift, brother, but you. Your mission was to scout beyond our lands, not to collect us a human sacrifice. Now, half our clan is missing on the horizon of this event," Dezetus raised a wooden lever and the wall opened. Heavy mist flooded in from the outside. Aldora looked beyond to find nothing but more of it distorting her view.

"You are not the chief anymore." Vedikus followed him.

"Neither are you!" Dezetus roared. Somewhere, far off in the distance, an animal howled back. Both minotaurs stopped and Aldora held her breath. The strain of this past fortnight had been threatening to boil over, as both suspected the other of being the reason why Hinekur and Thyrius had gone.

Aldora rushed over to Vedikus and placed her hand on his forearm, imploring him to stop. "He will never be satisfied unless he searches for them himself." The muscles under her fingers gradually loosened. "Let him go."

She glanced up to see Dezetus watching her.

"You may be precious, *human*, on this side of the wall, but understand, you are not one of us. Our mother taught us that well. You will never be one of us." He took a step toward her. "I will come back with my brothers, and when I do, we'll all know the truth." He turned to Vedikus. Her mate moved to step between them.

"No," she urged, squeezing his arm. Aldora walked back to the fire and picked up the wooden carving. Her fingers slid over the patches of smooth wood to the rougher areas that had yet to be finished. In her hand was a partially finished idol of a human woman. She carried it with her and handed it to Dezetus, hoping he would take it from her hand.

Vedikus growled menacingly as Dezetus narrowed his eyes upon her. She turned the idol in her hand and slowly, with heavy suspicion, Dezetus relieved her of it. Aldora wiped her palm on her cloak to hide the tremor. "I will prove you wrong," she said.

Dezetus snorted. "We shall see." His chest expanded and a trail of steam expelled from his nose.

Aldora nodded and returned to Vedikus's side, needing the distance.

"Brother," Dezetus looked at Vedikus, "I will return with our kin."

"Return with them." The anger in him had not abated. "Or do not return at all."

They shared a look of warning, of pent-up male aggression, and she knew then, that there was something she hadn't been told. A secret that the brothers shared that kept them together. If they battled, Aldora wouldn't know who would win. Her heart told her Vedikus but…

She shook her head, scrutinizing the two of them, trying to divest the tension that crackled between them. Dezetus glanced at her once more before turning away and stomping through the gate. The last thing she saw was the tip of his horn, before it too, was consumed by the mist.

Then, at last, her and Vedikus were once again alone. She moved past him and pulled the lever of the gate. It closed with finality and silence. The added strain of dealing with Dezetus's disgust while adapting to this new life had not been easy.

He will find his answers. Aldora stared, unmoving, at the black wood of the gate.

"Aldora, come and let us prepare for nightfall."

She turned to find Vedikus storming back to their nest. Her gaze sensually followed the hard outlines of his corded muscles, down the brown fur on his bull legs, and to his hooves that she loved to touch. He disappeared within and a smile lifted her lips when light bloomed from the cracks of the old stone windows. Her hands found her belly. Her skin warmed under her furs.

He's already inside me.

As she neared, the smell of blisterwood smoke and woodsy herbs filled her nose. She stopped for a moment to breathe it in, closing her eyes in pleasure and anticipation. *Yes.* Her fingers trailed over bandages on her palm. Aldora untied the cloak from her shoulders and let it drop to her feet, enjoying the mountain chill on her heated flesh.

Yes. Her eyes glazed over as she pushed the heavy flap of leather aside to enter.

Vedikus stood in the center of the space like a demon bathed in firelight, a creature not of her world, with a small bone dagger in his hand. His prick extruded from between his legs, dripping with lubrication. Surrounding him on the floor was a circle of crude design, red with their blood and willow growth, with pieces of blisterwood, all alight, placed in triangular patterns alongside it.

Aldora approached him slowly, to stand just outside the circle, where she stripped off the last of her clothes.

He reached for her when she stood naked before him and helped her across the threshold. Her sex leaked with essence down her thighs. The bandages were peeled from her hand and dropped to the floor. She shivered, swaying into his heat when he brought her delicate wound to his mouth and licked it thoroughly.

"Vedikus," she breathed his name, giving into the ritual, and the curse they both wanted to destroy. There was no mist here.

"Blood guard us, blood sustain, until the day that only blood remains."

Aldora bent down to grab the bull mask at her feet, and rose on her toes to place it over his head. It hung on him heavily, showing only his eyes.

"We will open the skies together," she said, tracing her gaze over his mask. "With our young."

"With our strength," he grunted, leaning in for a heretical kiss.

Author's Note

Thank you for reading Blooded, the first book that follows the Bestial Tribe Minotaurs. Keep an eye out for book two, coming in 2019, following one of the deliciously brutal brothers of the Bathyr clan. And if you liked the story or have a comment please leave me a review. I'd love to know your thoughts!

If you love cyborgs, aliens, anti-heroes, and adventure, follow me on facebook or through my blog online for information on new releases and updates.

Join my newsletter for the same information.

Naomi Lucas

Turn the page if you're wondering what I'm working on next...

Sneak Peek

Chaos Croc

Cyborg Shifters Book Six

Janet was a man eater.

She knew what men wanted, took what she pleased and used that to her advantage. But the men who lived in the small colonies on her home planet were not the same as those who traveled and conquered the universe. They were nothing like the Cyborgs who showed up to solve all her family's problems, especially the green-eyed god who crowded her space.

So she used him like she used the rest—and bit off far more than she could ever chew.

Zeph carried a demon on his back, one that scratched at the inside of his skull relentlessly. No one would guess that the neon green knight had a terrible secret, not with his charm and his lies. And because of his charisma, his razzle-dazzle darkness, the EPED used him for all he was worth. But sometimes missions can't be fixed with diplomacy. Sometimes you have to follow your own instincts—even a croc's instincts—to go after what you really want.

He wanted Janet. He wanted to keep her.

But the demon wanted something else entirely.

98728898R00171

Made in the USA
Lexington, KY
09 September 2018